From
Another
World

From Another World

Evelina Santangelo

Translated from the Italian by Ruth Clarke

GRANTA

Granta Publications, 12 Addison Avenue, London W11 4QR

First published in Great Britain by Granta Books, 2021

First published in Italy as *Da un altro mondo* in 2018 by
Giulio Einaudi editore, Torino.
This edition published by agreement with
Piergiorgio Nicolazzini Literary Agency (PNLA).

This book has been translated thanks to a translation grant awarded by the Italian
Ministry of Foreign Affairs and International Cooperation.

Questo libro è stato tradotto grazie a un contributo alla traduzione assegnato dal
Ministero degli Affari Esteri e della Cooperazione Internazionale italiano.

A CIP catalogue record for this book
is available from the British Library.

1 3 5 7 9 10 8 6 4 2

ISBN 978 1 78378 666 4
eISBN 978 1 78378 667 1

Typeset in Garamond by M Rules
Printed and bound by CPI Group (UK) Ltd, Croydon, CR0 4YY

For anyone who is not angry

We are facing unknown type if death ... But it's certainly death after everyone let us alone.

Rami Zayat, from the destroyed city of Aleppo

The best answer will come from the person who is not angry.

Arabic proverb

1

Sicily, 10 September 2020

'We'll be seeing the proverbial green mice when autumn comes around.' This ominous prediction was all anyone heard the harbourmaster say after the umpteenth sea rescue of an unconfirmed number of refugees, migrants, or whatever they were. But because he looked up at the sky as he said it, many of his men wondered whether he was talking about the unseasonably fickle weather, or the thankless work they were compelled to carry out night after night in their little corner of the ocean. 'The White Middle Sea' as it was called by the Arabs, who must know nothing about the sea, the harbourmaster thought, with the black water foaming before his eyes.

Most of the men were inclined towards the first theory – that the harbourmaster was talking about the weather – either because that autumn was genuinely unusual, or out of some kind of superstition, so as not to entertain even the idea of new shipwrecks, rescues, estimated lists of victims, and the whole corollary of risks and controversies: because they had done too much, because they hadn't done enough, because they should have done things in a completely different way, as if there were *a completely different way* to haul on board masses of slippery bodies flailing their arms and crashing against each other, so weak it seemed they were just souls.

2

Brussels, 10 September

A tormented soul, or something like that. That's what Khaled makes of the woman wandering the aisles of the discount store he'd sneaked into, to shelter from the rain. Sausaged up in a floral dress, she was staring into space in front of a display of chocolate treats. She hadn't even noticed the puddle of water that, a moment earlier, he had dripped onto that very same square of tiles, from trainers that felt like sunken boats and bare legs streaked with hair and mud.

He didn't like the way she suddenly jumped and turned to stare at him – like she'd seen a ghost. He hadn't done anything. He hadn't touched anything. He didn't even intend to accept the packet of biscuits the woman had pulled from the shelf and was offering to him with a deranged smile. Or maybe it was the neon light that was deranged.

Don't trust people who are too kind, or people who are too sad.

Then he thought, 'What the hell.' He gestured the woman over to the luggage section and pointed to a red wheeled suitcase at the top of the special offer shelf.

That was what he wanted, yes. He nodded. He didn't need anything else. And he had no intention of telling her his name, no matter how clearly she enunciated – or gesticulated – when she asked him, endeavouring to make herself understood.

He left the discount store with two bags full of stuff: new trainers, a pair of trousers, a checked shirt, a padded jacket and the packet of biscuits the woman had slipped under his arm.

Now, sitting in front of a fire that gives out nothing but smoke, in a lay-by beside the motorway, near a copse of scrawny trees, he feels bad for being so obstinate. The fact is, he doesn't want to go around telling people his name. 'The tree of silence bears the fruit of peace.' That's what his grandmother always said.

3

Brussels, 10 September

The moment she arrives home, automatically unlocking the front door and switching on the light, is always the worst part of the day for Karolina. Getting up in the morning is torture – not only because of the drugs that fill her head with cotton wool until lunchtime – but it's life, the hours that never seem to pass, the sixty seconds counted out by clock hands piecing together a full minute, the very idea of all that empty time between waking and sleep, that turns her brain to mush.

Treading carefully on a carpet that only bears a trace of its true colours at the corners, Karolina approaches the room where she will go through the customary motions. She will knock and wait for an answer, then, asking permission, she will turn the handle, quickly welcoming the sight of the picture window large enough to capture the light still filtering through the milky white sky.

Today, though, things are a little better than usual. It was a good idea to buy those spiced biscuits to put on the desk between the kickboxing gloves and the computer she had recently put back in its place.

She doesn't know whether she should leave the bed like this, with just the light duvet tucked tight at the corners, or arrange the yellow cushions along the wall. *How to turn a bed into a sofa* the online sewing lesson was called. Successfully completing that one small task had, for a while, given some meaning to her days.

When she finally makes her decision, she feels a sort of relief. The yellow goes well with the moss green on the wall, even though it's covered with stickers and posters of rock bands, or punk rock bands, or who knows what. Stuff that fries your brain – that's what she'd say now if anyone asked her. And opening the box of biscuits and arranging a few on a saucer beside a cup of black tea is another sensible decision.

At least that way, when she closes the door behind her, leaving the room to drift into the late afternoon, there is a lovely smell of cinnamon, ginger, cloves, cardamom and nutmeg. It stays with her on the few steps that separate her son's room from the kitchen where she will end up shuffling around until it is time for her to face the night, stuffed full of pills that simulate sleep.

4

Palermo, 11 September

'Rats!' thought the beach cleaner, staring at the shore.

The forecasts had promised storms, with a sirocco wind in the south and on the island of Sicily. And sure enough, as soon as dawn broke, patches of metallic grey began to emerge like bruises in the cobalt-blue sky.

The pearly white sand was speckled, that September day, with tracks that bore all the signs of being the footprints of a small mammal, or perhaps, as investigators would later speculate, a bird. 'Rats!' The cleaner was in no doubt. People changing the story like that annoyed him. Especially since he had no talent for anything else, if the truth be told. But he was a 'specialist', a *refuse collection operative*, and he knew what he was talking about.

It wasn't so much the shape that caught his eye, perhaps because of the gusts of wind flattening the sand, but the sheer quantity. As though a horde of rats had cascaded onto the shore. Or a flock of migrating birds had decided to stop there, without leaving any other trace, 'not a feather, not even the distant echo of chirping', a local journalist would report later, rather poetically.

The fact is that, watching the indigo sea roll as the gusts of wind picked up, you got the feeling that the hordes of rats, or

birds, or who knows what that nobody had seen, those count-
less entities, had been finally transformed by magic into bright
white crests that foamed out to sea, on the way to Tunisia, Libya,
Algeria or even Morocco.

Just sipping a coffee in front of that spectacle, the swirling
sand letting itself be drawn towards the electric call of the sea,
was all it took for the cleaner to abandon his ideas and specu-
lation – at least until the day he overheard the guard on duty
outside the bank, who had nothing much to report, except the
fact that that night, by the sea, it hadn't felt as hot.

'That's it?'

'That's it.'

5

Brussels, 11 September

Since he'd untangled himself from his mother's embrace on the doorstep, precisely three years ago, the only person he'd really been able to depend on, whenever he caught himself thinking, 'I'd be better off dead,' was Padre Buono, the Good Father. That's what the boys on the building site called him, even though there was nothing good about him. In fact, as Khaled's brother said, he was the biggest shit of all, the way he said, 'You, yes; you, no,' and with a smack on the head he'd send the 'yeses' off to work. But then, at the end of the day, he always paid up. And he remembered everyone's name, even Khaled's brother, who would wait all day at the site entrance, making a game out of throwing stones into puddles or into a broken plaster bucket.

He said, 'Bastard,' and, 'Son of a bitch,' and, 'What the fuck are you doing?', but if boys were willing to learn, he would always keep them on. Maybe with a boot to the head occasionally; anything goes if someone's up to no good.

Even now, if Khaled puts a hand on the back of his neck, in one particular spot, it still hurts. But the whole time he was working on the site, he never spent a single night sleeping outside the hut – and nor did his brother. Same mattress, same covers.

It's good to sleep in pairs when it's freezing outside, he thinks,

looking for the sun's halo through the dead branches. It's good
to have someone by your side who can do the job right.

'Let's do this job right!' That was what Padre Buono had shouted
at him a few days earlier, yanking him back, when Khaled didn't
want to hear a word about them dropping the bar on the ground.
He'd started yelling, 'I'll kill you all!' And he would have done it,
too, if that bastard Padre Buono hadn't grabbed his wrist, forcing
him down onto his knees beside his brother's body and the iron
bar that had crashed from the fourth floor.

'It's the kid's own fault,' the boys said. He'd slipped through
the site entrance and sat right under the scaffolding. They'd seen
the girder plough through the air. The thud on the ground had
been so unremarkable that at first no one even noticed. 'You go
and get it.' 'No, you!' Nobody had wanted to climb all the way
down and back up. After all, who would have imagined it? That's
what they kept repeating with horror in their eyes, stammering,
trying to explain themselves to Padre Buono.

Only occasionally would Khaled shift his fierce gaze towards
his brother, lying there, staring up at the sky. 'Who the hell
would have thought that the little prick would have gone and
sat there?' he heard someone hiss.

Padre Buono gave them an angry wave that seemed to say,
'Piss off!' Then 'Let's do this job right ... All right, boy?' he
repeated, squeezing Khaled's arm even tighter. And he fell to his
knees. Not because his wrist hurt, he didn't give a fuck that his
wrist hurt. It was the way that bastard Padre Buono said those
last words that exposed the raw nerve of his rage.

'All right?'

For hours, in the deserted hut, crouching in a corner between
the camp beds, Khaled watched Padre Buono busying himself at
a table with water and gauze: disinfecting, cleaning his brother's

arms, legs and chest – lying there bare it looked like the breast of a sparrow. His lifeless features, wearing none of the smirks and funny faces that always drove his mother crazy when it was bath time and he would run through the whole house in his underpants.

His mother would certainly have been proud to see her son clean and tidy, and smelling nice. That thought had come into his stupid head, as the strong smell of camphor rose up through his nostrils.

Rubbing away a tear with the back of his hand, Khaled stands up, and looks at the halo around the low sun, glinting through the cobweb of branches. He pulls the suitcase close. It takes him a while to figure out how to unfasten the clasp to open it, then he peers inside, at the pearly grey lining.

He kicks himself for not having thought to pick up scissors or a sharp knife.

6

Brussels, 11 September

Ever since she opened her eyes, Karolina has been thinking about it. She was still thinking about it as she splashed cold water on her face, and drank her sole cup of coffee, before she dashed across the patch of grass in front of the house, and into the dark street dotted with shadowy figures. They looked even lonelier in the glare of the street lamps marking the way to the metro station some two kilometres away.

She hates her job, but that morning she'd put an unusual amount of energy into vacuuming the carpet at the estate agency before the others arrived – the people who only ransack everything that she, between five and eight every morning, puts back to rights, leaving behind an expanse of glass panels and geometrically aligned desks, all clean and tidy.

Quite the opposite of what she can see now, reflected in the carriage window: a puffy face framed by three strands of hair that have escaped from her hairclip and look greasy even through the fingerprints smeared on the glass. She is so tired that she could just go home and flop onto the sofa, were it not for that one thought: going back to the shopping centre.

When she finally arrives, she sits on a bench and waits. She was right to put two woollen coats over her flannel dress, though they must make her look like an old bag lady. At this hour the cold is biting, even on a clear day like this.

She waits. She watches the sales assistants gather by the entrance as the shutters rise with a horrible clanking of chains. She waits.

Now that the discount store has been open for a good half an hour, she knows she can't stay sitting there for long. After a while, the security guard will come over. He will ask, 'Is everything all right, madam?' with that cold kindness that invites her to move along.

Just as the security guard squashes his cigarette butt into the ashtray, Karolina decides to stand up.

Same aisle as yesterday. Same display of biscuits, cereals and waffles, some heart-shaped, for a 'sweet breakfast', according to a flyer that drifts to the ground.

On the other side, past the display, she thinks she can make out her reason for being there, in that particular spot, at that particular time.

'Did you eat the biscuits?' Karolina asks the person she thinks might be the boy with the red suitcase. 'Biscuits,' she repeats to no avail, walking around the shelf and holding up the packet in an attempt to get at least a nod out of him.

She is happy to see the boy wearing the padded jacket, even if his legs are still bare and dirty. She is also happy that he takes this new packet of cookies out of her hand, nodding. She's only sorry she has no way to feel whether his hands are cold – contact that would take her back to the only intimate gesture she'd had left with her son. A special form of tenderness, of which Karolina had always been very proud: before she left for work at dawn, she would take Andreas's hands from the bed, and kiss them while he slept. She never woke him once.

She couldn't say how many times she'd visited the aisles of the discount store just to catch the boy, who always stays one step behind her and never opens his mouth. Nor how long she stands watching him walk away, dragging a luggage trolley stacked with packaged food – the only thing it seemed he couldn't do without, along with the large scissors from the sale aisle.

Today she did manage to find out his name, although she gets the feeling that there won't be a next time. She keeps pondering this as she stares deep into the mist rolling across the fallow fields, beyond the wall where she finally lost sight of Khaled.

Karolina would remember that September day for months. Partly because it made her happy just to think about that lost little boy. Partly because it explained events she'd never have dreamed she'd be caught up in.

7

Palermo, 16 September

Short circuits and power surges had been the order of the day for some time there, on the outskirts of the city.

Some people said it was just the latest in a long list of signs that the neighbourhood had been abandoned, and others claimed that the residents were to blame. 'They're people who're hardwired to break the law, and you just know they wouldn't think twice about tapping into the electricity network . . .' These were the rumours on the local estates, where weeds and railings marked borders impenetrable to prying eyes, but not to the skilled hands of burglars who, some weekends, would venture as far out as the most abandoned, most notorious fringes of the district.

The Zona Espansione Nord – Northern Expansion Zone – known as the Zen, was like a channel between the far reaches of the city and the first towns and villages before Mondello, with its stately promenade and its beach, so pearly white that no one would ever have imagined its history as a swamp, or 'muddy port'. *Marsā 'at Tin*, the Arabs called it.

Perhaps it was because of the coast's aristocratic overtones, but no one realised that these tiny, momentary short circuits were generated by the old swamp itself and only at a later stage did they hit the dormitory neighbourhood of the Zen, with its high-rise islands: little stacked fortresses of miserable, shabby boxes. The plaster started coming down as soon as the construction work ended, and now there was nothing to do but patch up the deepest of the cracks that, in some places, split open walls inside the houses.

There, among thick smoke rising from the heaps of abandoned rubbish, it wasn't easy for the kids to understand exactly how things happened that Mediterranean autumn afternoon, on the square of cement and weeds they had chosen as a football pitch. 'The Clearing', that's what everyone called it, from the day they learned to walk on their own two feet.

They sweated like mad: they knew that much.

That afternoon, there was a muggy African heat that made the buildings look even yellower. The sweat mixed with mud from the dubious puddles they all shoved each other into, because this was the last game of the summer season, before the winter tournament started, even though many of them were more inclined to think of it as a between-season tournament, 'the changeover', as it was known. Really, everyone had their own name for it. And no one minded. Playing was all that mattered.

Despite the heat, the mud, the smoke, what unfolded between 4.00 p.m. and 8.00 p.m. that September day was a legendary game that would go down in the history books of the Clearing, where, at around 7.30 p.m., on top of everything, all the street lamps lit up. 'Like San Siro!' said the older kids, who had been intent on stressing the epic scale of this game for days. 'Not eleven against eleven,' someone ventured, 'but fifty against fifty, or even five hundred against five hundred!'

The number of goals was also so high that people lost count – something like 100 to 150. As if the entire Zen neighbourhood were playing: dads, cousins, brothers in prison, and even more, as expressed by one little boy who spread his arms out wide to indicate the universe. Something he would swear on, confiding in a cousin who lived at the other end of the city, among the palatial buildings and dilapidated facades of the historic centre, in an alley with its sign written in two languages, Italian and some floaty script that looked like Arabic, even though no one spoke either.

He said, 'Oh, the other night, at the Clearing, we played with, like, the rest of the world.'

'What does that mean?'

'I don't know, but I can swear on it!'

And as he swore, he spat three times on the ground.

8

Brussels, 16 September

His mouth tastes like a mixture of dirt and moss. He opens his eyes wide, terrified. He must have had a nightmare. But his suitcase is still there. He'd had his legs clamped around it all night long. He must have kicked and screamed at some point, because his throat is dry and his body is dotted with little clumps of moss. One of his blankets has ended up in a puddle half a metre away, while the other, knotted like a knapsack, is still close by. He'd held it tight against his chest, gently resting his head on it.

Before getting up and looking around, Khaled moves his makeshift pillow delicately, the way you'd handle a fragile object. He sees nothing around him. Only a mist with wiry branches poking through. If he were a baby, they would have scared him. Fear was another thing his brother called 'shitty'. But with fear, the more you think about it, the stronger it gets, the more it sucks the energy out of you, and he has a lot of things to do, before the trucks arrive and someone gets out to take a leak or stretch their legs. That's what had happened yesterday. Fortunately, he'd had time to duck into the bushes.

The palms of his hands are dirty, and he leaves long black streaks on the bright red suitcase where he tries to wipe the frost off the plastic. He doesn't want to waste the little bit of water left in his bottle. 'Match your stride to the length of your carpet,' was his grandmother's motto. But he should at least use some to give his hands a wash, and a bit for his face, and a bit for the suitcase. And he should drink a few sips. There'll be enough for all that, and even some to tidy up his hair.

His mother had put a mother-of-pearl comb in his pocket, and he has been careful not to lose it. He hadn't realised how much his hair had grown since the last time Padre Buono cut it. He'd let him do it, sitting on the stool, perfectly still and silent, even when the blade passed dangerously close to his eye and then his neck. 'You'll go far, boy,' Padre Buono told him when he was finished, pushing him off the stool. 'Next!' The kid after him in the queue didn't have a hair on his head. He stared at the blade. He looked like the lamb they'd slaughtered in secret so they could have a proper meal, just for one day. Padre Buono laughed, forcing the boy onto the stool. 'For you, the works. We'll skin you, and that'll be that!'

His mother would surely have laughed if she could see him. And what if she could see him from across the sea? In a dream, maybe. She'd tell him, just like she told him before he left, 'Putting a comb through your hair costs nothing.' Which followed on from another thought: 'You can tell someone cares about their children if they're washed and have their hair combed every morning.'

He doesn't know if it's really his mother guiding him, but he feels he should do things properly before he sets off. He washes his hands and face, then puts on the trousers and shirt he was given by the woman at the discount store. Not the jacket and shoes, though. He'll do that later.

He picks up the blanket that landed in the puddle, folds it, kneels down and tries to arrange everything in the suitcase. It's big enough inside, now that Khaled has cut the grey lining. He feels a bit bad about it, but he had no choice. He'd been right to get a case that was neither too big nor too small.

With a burst of energy, he arranges the suitcase on the trolley, then takes a few minutes to admire his work. He's pleased he chose a bright red that stands out, even in the middle of the fog.

Anyone passing by that day would have seen a skinny little boy, no more than thirteen years old, wandering around a lay-by with a few scrawny trees just off the motorway. But the care with which Khaled puts on his padded jacket and the new trainers, leaving the old ones beside the embers of a dying fire, gives the impression of someone who always makes sure they're properly turned out before they leave the house.

When the first lorry driver pulls into the area, just for a stretch and some fresh air, the thing that catches his eye is a flash of red, bobbing up and down in the milky distance, and not much else.

The tricks tiredness plays on you, when you've notched up too many hours behind the wheel, day and night.

9

Brussels, 16 September

There isn't even any sign of the local police these days. Seven months earlier, when Karolina and her ex-husband decided to report Andreas missing, the house had turned into a port, with people coming and going at all hours – local police, federal police, special units – when she really wanted to be left alone to collect the thoughts that were swirling around in her head, to bleach them from her mind. The more she said, 'I can't remember,' or 'I don't know,' the more they persisted. His friends, the music he did or did not listen to, any vices he had or had given up, whether he'd changed, and how much. Those were the kinds of questions they insisted on after turning Andreas's room upside down without finding what they were looking for, not even the laptop.

'What can you tell me about this? Do you know anything about this?' an officer asked at one point. He was middle-aged and must have been of Turkish origin, or something like that. He was showing her a T-shirt with a fighter's face set inside a shield with 'Zero Tolerance' written across the top. And underneath, in block capitals as if carved into stone, WHITE REX.

'Do you know what we're talking about?'

Karolina shook her head silently.

'Then let me tell you. These here are swastikas and this is a Black Sun,' the officer explained, pointing to the shield. 'Those things in the two eagles' beaks are more hooked crosses, and there's a nice knuckleduster in the middle. Are you with me now?'

She took off her glasses, and brought her eyes close to the shield.

'He hadn't worn that for ages. Or at least ... I don't remember him wearing it ...' she whispered, as the officer started in on the boy's hair.

'All right, let's move on,' interrupted one of the federal police officers, with the air of someone who felt his job was being done for him.

Not that it made any difference. 'So, how did he wear it? Long, short, shaved? How did he have it?' the Turkish officer repeated, breathing into her face.

'Şahin ... Ramazan Şahin ...' one of the local police said, using his full name in an attempt to calm him down.

'A bit like yours, lately,' Karolina answered, just for something to say, given how many times her son changed the length, cut and sometimes even colour of his hair.

'What are you doing? Are you taking the piss?' retorted the cranky Turkish officer. He tapped something into his phone and showed her a frightening video on the screen.

A hail of shrapnel, ash, explosions, the skeleton of a wooden boat aground in fetid waters, derelict buildings, hooded soldiers with machine guns on their backs, more explosions, fire and flames, armoured tanks, black flags, hooded protesters, police clashes and words fired onto the screen covering the bullets shooting in the background. Dominating everything, a wolf-like voice, digging up words from a pit full of bodies.

'We took this from a Facebook profile that was most likely

created by your son. *No judge, inciting hatred, no God or the butcher God of their bastard dreams.* That's what Slaughter to Prevail say they want . . . massacres, bloodshed, butchery, slaughter . . .' The officer was getting worked up while she listened, stunned, failing to see the purpose of frightening her like this. After all, she was only asking for help. But the officer, for reasons she couldn't fathom, insisted on showing her a second video.

More shrapnel and ash, but this time against a confused backdrop of bodies: hooded boys shouting, throwing objects, stretching out their arms in Nazi salutes. Writing that must be extremely violent. In Cyrillic.

'And this is You Must Murder's "Evil Russia". Millions of views and shares, including some by your son.'

Karolina noticed a quiver of the man's lips, but otherwise his face seemed carved in stone.

'But what has my son got to do with the Russians? What – could he speak—?' she spluttered.

'He must have understood enough.' The officer silenced her, his purple face showing the look of someone who has a score to settle: with her, with Andreas, or with one of those boys in the video throwing smoke bombs and objects in the midst of Nazi salutes.

'I don't think he understood a word of Russian,' Karolina muttered.

'You don't think what? *You* don't think *what?*'

'That on his computer there was . . .'

'The fact is there's no sign of either of them, not your son and not the computer!' the officer shouted, sounding as though Andreas had wronged him personally.

'I think you're going too far,' interrupted a colleague from who knows which police force, taking him by the arm. 'Come on.'

'And do you think these guys are worried about going too far?' the Turkish officer muttered, allowing the other agent to escort him out of the room, still sharing details of a neo-Nazi skinhead raid.

Karolina could hear that he was talking about his own son, or perhaps she could just tell from the way the officer shrank into his shoulders when he finished.

'Do you understand what these *nice boys* do? People have practically got themselves killed, getting involved with scum like that.'

They were interrupted by the sharp voice of a caseworker, or she could have been a psychologist, or another one of the investigation team, but in plain clothes.

'I'm sorry about his son . . .' was all Karolina could say, staring at the door after the man. Then she froze up.

'I'm sorry, but you, what did *you* know about your son, Andreas? I mean . . .'

Karolina didn't hear what she *meant*.

'He liked cookies,' was her only response, her mind going up in flames.

'Now you *are* taking the piss!' exclaimed the woman, who must have had an entirely different theory to the Turkish officer. 'Your son, last summer, he worked at a shop on rue de Ribaucourt, not far from the Mevlana Mosque, is that right?'

Karolina put the palm of her hand to her forehead as she struggled to comprehend the pieces of this newly described geography, which took her to an altogether different part of the city.

'I don't know. I don't think so. No.'

'And yet I think he did,' the woman insisted, giving her a searching look that she found exasperating.

'Why don't you ask *him*?' Karolina cried, turning to her ex-husband, trying to escape another barrage of questions.

She staggered out of the room. 'I just want you to find *my son*,' were her final words.

'The problem is knowing *where he is*! And *who* the hell he is!' snapped the caseworker, or psychologist, or plain-clothes officer – whatever she was, she wasn't keeping it together.

That night, Karolina's ex-husband came to the bedroom doorway in the dark. From the depths of that darkness, he launched a verbal attack. It wasn't the words that terrified her, but his creepy, distorted voice.

'You *know* he and I haven't seen each other for months! You know that, don't you? So what can I possibly *know* about what your son got up to? What kind of people he was hanging out with? Now I'm the one who's supposed to answer the questions . . . What the hell have I got to do with *Nazis*, or . . . with the *allah akbar* from the shop? You fucking halfwit!'

The kick he aimed at the bed made her curl into a ball, despite the fact she was a sturdy woman.

Lying still with her eyes wide open, she expected things to go the way they always had, before she found the courage to 'save herself', as her friend Fenna put it. But instead, the voice disappeared back into the darkness as quickly as it had exploded.

Only once she had heard the door slam violently did she close her eyes, exhausted, toying with the idea that Andreas had come back just in time to throw his father out of the house.

Now, months had passed with no progress.

A few nights ago, Karolina had felt a violent shiver run down her spine. Listening to a television programme about Brussels – 'the capital of Flanders, of Belgium and of Europe', the pretentious voice-over announced – she discovered that the original name of the settlement of Bruxella, Brocela, Bruolisela, or whatever the hell her city had been called, meant 'village on the swamp'.

How do you go about finding a boy who has sunk into the swamp?

10

Palermo, 18–29 September

There was much slamming of doors and desks, and a frantic scurrying along the corridors on that first day of school when the rumours started to fly.

The neighbourhood was in an almost central area of the city. Beautiful tree-lined streets where pretty little buildings and gardens from the thirties alternated with exclusive condominiums, illegally approved and illegally built, evoking the time when they came to be owned – between shipments of explosives and conveniently timed fires – by developers, politicians and surveyors, whose grandchildren, or great-grandchildren, together with the children of other professionals, now attended schools where everyone knew which rung of the local middle classes a particular surname could reach. All of which made schools like that 'some of the safest' in the city, and places there some of the most sought-after.

The first to raise the issue were teachers with years of experience under their belts, so many that they could identify every smudge, hole or smear on the walls, just as they could the changes in the human landscape.

'Suspicious movements'. They couldn't agree on a better phrase to define a 'notable presence' of faces they had never seen before, mixed in with familiar or half-familiar faces, which tended to appear in the youngest classes, in particular.

One of the newly appointed teachers, that is to say one who had transferred to this outstanding school no more than a year ago, argued that all this fuss seemed rather alarmist. That they were, after all, at the beginning of the school year, and they still needed to commit pupils' names and faces to memory. The deputy head preferred this second theory, which seemed sensible, obvious even.

After a couple of weeks, two camps formed within the teaching body: 'veterans' and 'newbies'. A conflict erupted between the old guard who were trying to make the case for the benefit of experience, and the vanguard defending the argument of plausibility.

Since the headteacher had not decided to take any measures with regard to the 'strange goings on' in the student population, and since there was now a war between the two positions that exaggerated or reduced how much the number of children varied from one hour to the next, and the size of the crowds recorded at break time, the deputy head – who represented the middle ground, having arrived recently but holding the necessary authority – had all the morning registers sent to her.

Gathering the classes in the gym, she tried taking a whole group register, which clearly showed an excessive number of hands raised for certain similar surnames, barely recognisable over the deafening chatter, with some kids throwing their hands up at random, creating total confusion.

A class council meeting, called with the utmost urgency, brought up the word 'gypsy'.

One of the teachers also ventured that, between lessons, children were actually sneaking in through the windows. Yet there was no way in heaven or earth that could be true, since children like that – gypsy, or Romani, or whatever – had to be dragged in from home, from the *camps*, or left there, end of story.

Ideas like this were not based on any kind of experience. That school had never seen a single Romani child. Moreover, none of the children had anything unusual to report, apart from the post-summer weirdness of finding themselves stuck behind a desk for hours on end. Nor had anyone reported stolen pencil cases or jackets, only a few snacks or pencils later discovered in their neighbour's backpack.

'Physiological appropriations' the headteacher called them. She thought it irresponsible to spread rumours along the lines of 'possible raids on *undocumented* pupils' within the walls of a school that 'made safety one of its selling points'.

Refusing to give in to the arrogance of those who scoffed at the stories, one teacher with some artistic skills tried to draw her most faithful identikit sketches of a couple of faces that 'clearly', as she stressed, did not belong to the student body. The head-teacher slipped these well-crafted charcoal portraits into her desk drawer – in the vain hope that time would do its job and fade the drawings completely – until she was forced to dig them out.

This happened when one of the parents appeared in the head's office first thing in the morning. His son had been refusing to bring books and folders to school for days. 'Like them,' the child had said, wild-eyed, stamping his feet and throwing his backpack out of the window.

'Them, who?'

'Them, the ones sitting on the teacher's desk, under the desk, on the windowsills. And sometimes they fly,' he added, moving his hand like an aeroplane crashing into the ground.

11

Brussels, 18–19 September

He's lost track of how many hours he's been walking. The dirt track that runs alongside the motorway is full of holes. His wrist hurts from dragging the trolley, laden with his suitcase and the bags of food. It leans from one side to the other, constantly making him twist his arm. It's lucky he's got such comfortable shoes with all that rubber under his feet. What worries him are all the cars speeding by on the other side of the guard rail. Especially the articulated lorries. Every time one goes past, and there are so many, he feels a rumble behind him and then a vacuum.

Even though he's not someone who gets tired, he really wants to sit down for a few minutes by this time, at least to shake the dirt out of his shoes. But he can't. He's got to get to the next service area and find the lay-by where the direct bus to the south usually stops for a break, or so he's been told. They'd written the exact kilometre marker on a piece of paper.

He has his own way, Khaled, of staving off tiredness. A trick that never worked with Nadir, in fact it had the opposite effect. His brother whined even more when he said, 'Come on, what's the nicest thing you can think of?' At that point Nadir wouldn't be able to contain himself and would burst into tiny, desperate sobs. There was no way to console him. Baby stuff. That doesn't happen with Khaled any more.

He grits his teeth and keeps walking into what passes for the sun, making its way slowly to the horizon. He starts to think about the last nice thing he saw. The golden buildings in the Grand Place on Christmas night. Pink and purple lights climbing up the walls. Buildings that seemed to be made of ice, or sculpted from multicoloured stone. There was one in particular that was suddenly crowded with pixies, *jinn* running up and down and up and down, crazy for the lights and the music. 'Lucifer!' Nadir whispered, his eyes widening. He must have heard his mother use that word. The people were crazy, too, so tightly packed with their noses in the air as if they were on a giant carousel with the music getting louder and louder. It seemed to move from one building to the next, from one colour to the next. And there they were, spinning around with the buildings. He lost count of how many cups of mulled wine they'd been given by a guy from the building site who wanted to pay for everyone's drinks that night. Even Nadir had glazed eyes and a dark red moustache above his lip. He kept saying, 'Cinnamon, cinnamon,' as he zigzagged around pointing at the steaming paper cups. He wanted another sip.

They'd spent all the money from their pay packet on mulled wine, candied nuts, waffles topped with mountains of cream, and chips, piles of chips with tons of sauce. In the end, they felt drunk from head to toe, and kind of happy.

Happiness, according to Khaled, if you can hold on to it, will always attract something good. Like a magnet.

For example, the fact that he has now practically reached the service area seems, to him, to have something to do with those nice thoughts he'd managed to root out as he clocked up the last kilometres. And that he can treat himself to a pear juice, sitting on the steps of the bar. He would never have dared hope as much, but someone even offers him a lift.

It seems strange only in the way the man looks at him, laughing, when he takes the piece of paper from his pocket to show him which kilometre he needs to get to.

'In you get, go on!' he says, hopping into the mammoth truck that turns bright blue as soon as he puts the key in the ignition. The asphalt turns blue too!

'Get comfortable. There's a way to go!'

Khaled isn't the slightest bit comfortable, with the suitcase on his lap, but he has no intention of letting it go, not even when the man reaches out a hand to put it behind his seat, with the trolley.

'As if I'd want to steal it off you!'

He doesn't know how it happened, but he must have nodded off. When he opens his eyes, his head is leaning to one side and his arms are empty. He turns to the man, even more bewildered in the bluish hue that has come over the cabin, now that it is night-time.

'I put it there,' the guy says, pointing behind the seat. His face is barely visible in the phosphorescent light that scrambles his features. Khaled contorts himself, like a creature in a tiny cage, to grab the suitcase and put it back on his lap.

'What you got in there, gold nuggets?'

Now all he wants is to not be in the cabin of this mammoth truck in the middle of the night, on a motorway going who knows where. He takes the piece of paper from his pocket and looks at the meaningless street signs. He doesn't know what time it is, if it's deep in the night or just before dawn. He curses himself – he was a dick to fall asleep. The bluish darkness confuses him even more.

'Time to pee,' the man says at one point, bringing the

mammoth into a small lay-by past a tangle of bushes that only become visible when the beam of the headlamps hits them.

'Get out, kid!' He hears the driver's voice from the street, through the door, which suddenly opens and Khaled almost tumbles out.

'Get out!'

Khaled feels something clasp his arm. Some violent force grabs him and his suitcase, which falls to the ground. He doesn't even have time to bend down and pick it up before the man is in front of him, legs apart. His open fly in his face, a hand pressing on his head.

'This is how you pay me.' His jaw is clenched in an expression Khaled recognises immediately.

Padre Buono punched anyone in the head if they tried to pull something like this. Someone even got hit with a crowbar, down there, where Khaled is now kicking, frenzied, squirming. Then he does it: he takes the scissors from his jacket pocket. He has no intention of ending up like his friend Hakan, who carked it after they'd made it through the desert together, when they finally reached the coast.

'Don't touch me,' he says in his head. 'Don't touch me.' He backs away from the man, never lowering the blade, ready to leap forward and kill him like a dog. That's what he thinks, that he'll kill him like a dog if he takes one step.

'Bastard! Son of a bitch! Scumbag! Poof!'

But Khaled has already picked up his suitcase. He feels so strong when he sees the blade of the scissors glint in the headlights. Stronger than Padre Buono beating the shit out of someone with his iron bar.

12

Brussels, 18 September

Cleaning at the agency was more exhausting than usual this morning, or maybe it's just that she's more tired.

Even so, she wouldn't mind going to see her friend Fenna, the only person she feels she can share things with.

She's always told Fenna everything, which, given how life has turned out, has largely meant confiding in her about things that never went the way she imagined. And when she kicked out 'Andreas's father', as she called him in those days, she'd found an ally in Fenna, who could give her the right advice, tell her what she needed to hear to muster up the courage.

'Look at him, though! With his potato head. He can't do anything but talk big and make his point with his fists. Big talk, big hands, zero balls! Dickhead, dickhead, dickhead,' she'd clucked, imitating him. She'd even managed to make her laugh.

Now Karolina needs some more advice, or at least the comfort of someone who knows how to listen.

'It's not like anyone's going to end up in prison for shit like that these days!' Fenna had said when she told her the story about the Turkish officer whose son was beaten up by neo-Nazis, the one who was angry with Andreas and his T-shirts.

'It's not like anyone could be accused of being an alcoholic for wearing a T-shirt like mine, for example ...' She pointed to the line of increasingly fuzzy beer bottles, blurred by alcohol. 'And that's coming from someone who drinks, you know,' she spluttered.

Because Fenna has a quality that Karolina really appreciates. She's sincere. She has the guts to tell it how it is, even when that means acknowledging a vice that, several years earlier, had seen her on the verge of an alcohol-induced coma. 'They're phases, anyway,' she concluded. 'People make mistakes. Especially when they're still naive and don't know how shit life can be.'

In Karolina's case, after the last visit from the police, the problem was understanding what particular brand of shit her son had got himself into.

At first she had thought Andreas's disappearance was 'strategic', a way of getting out of some sort of trouble. Cash borrowed and not returned, or ill-gotten gains. She'd never uttered the words 'dealer' or 'loan shark', even though they had sometimes occurred to her.

'Mind your own business!' was her son's response, on the rare occasions she'd tried to ask him whether he needed any money. 'Do I need any money ...? I need a whole shedload. Have you got it?'

It still hurts, the dismissive smile he'd given her.

The day before she reported Andreas missing, she'd left the computer with Fenna, 'to look after for a while' she said.

She just didn't want strangers poking around in her son's things, that's all, she explained.

'It might be best if I stick it in the basement, though.'

'Won't it get cold?' Karolina said, without thinking.

'Then we'll put a blanket over it,' Fenna replied in her raspy voice, putting an arm around her.

And with that, they'd said all there was to say.

*

Fenna hadn't asked any questions a few days ago either, when Karolina decided to take Andreas's computer home.

She wasn't expecting any more searches now. It had been over a month since she'd seen anyone.

At first, though, it had taken her aback when Fenna said, 'If I were you, I wouldn't even turn it on.'

She couldn't believe Fenna would do that: betray her trust. Knowing her friend must have gone through everything on the computer, it was like knowing she'd slipped into her son's bed.

'Still, kids . . . if you really want to know, in the end you'll find out what they're up to,' Fenna added, handing her the laptop the same way she'd entrusted it to her, in a perfectly packaged box.

Maybe it's the sudden memory of that phrase; maybe it's the bright, late-autumn morning; or even harsher, maybe it's the sharp voice of that psychologist, or caseworker, or whatever she was: 'Your son, last summer, he worked at a shop on rue de Ribaucourt, not far from the Mevlana Mosque . . .' Maybe it's the fact that she can't stand the idea of herself sinking into the swamp of the city, with its thousand districts of this or that municipality, local police, federal police, Flemish, Walloon . . . but today she feels she has to do it: cross the Charleroi canal and try to ascertain with her own eyes – ascertain what, she really doesn't know.

As she crosses one of the bridges, she notices the beautiful, bold colours of the graffiti covering the canal walls. A crocodile, a child, a kind of satyr or a devil with a severed head, a skull, a squid: they seem to slide along at the slow pace of a pair of boats on the water. Even the plastic windmills, fixed along the railings of what must once have been a quay and is now a wide footpath, have a festive feel as they spin lazily outside former warehouses, depots and tower blocks, now fully refurbished, unrecognisable among the brick facades of the old working-class district of Molenbeek-Saint-Jean.

Going back to see the jade-coloured sailing boat on waves that reach the second floor of a slanted building, a perfectly insignificant structure but for the foaming sea and unfurled sails, Karolina walks a good way down quai des Charbonnages, and through place Saint-Jean Baptiste. Until a few years ago, she would sometimes buy harissa or cous cous around there. She never imagined that she would find the square deserted, with the church seeming even whiter, petrified, in front of the churchyard.

She turns back into rue de la Prospérité, where the only things thriving are the tufts of grass sprouting between the cracks in the pavement. High on the black-stained walls, all the windows are boarded up. It's the same in Gemeenteplaats. There isn't a single fruit and veg stall below the uniquely spectacular green dome of the Maison Communale, and the flags on the front are rolled up.

What baffles her more than anything, though, is the silence that hangs over the closed shops, as if the neighbourhood had been cleared out overnight: people, goods and property. There is just one man, floating around in black clothing, maybe a jalabiya, she couldn't say, heading towards her. He has a kind of peaceful expression, but his face looks entirely out of place in the ghostly surroundings. He is staring ahead, even though, apart from Karolina, there isn't a living soul on this stretch of road. She can't tell whether he's happy to have the neighbourhood so quiet, or whether he's waiting for the silence to explode.

Only in rue de l'École, through a window pane, does Karolina catch a glimpse of a woman's face, half covered by a heavy curtain or a veil. She's looking at her, maybe she's watching her, or maybe she's just waiting for the little boy who pops up in the middle of the street, pelting towards the front door, which slams and is left crooked on its hinges.

'Cockroaches,' mumbles a man Karolina hadn't noticed. 'Cockroaches should be gassed,' he keeps repeating to himself, in Flemish. He follows on her heels, while she tries, as quickly as she can, to find rue de Ribaucourt and the shop where they said Andreas had worked.

'And first: them!' the man goes on, still behind her. 'Gassed, all of them!' he repeats, breathing down her neck. 'They shut them down! Because of those terrorists.' He lets out a nervous laugh. 'And where, do you think? Right in my street!' he yells, coming up alongside Karolina, who is trying not to look at him.

'If you turn that corner, you're there. You'll see! They boarded up the ones on rue de Ribaucourt! There, right there!' he exclaims, pointing in the direction Karolina is headed.

'Can you hear that?' he asks, looking up to the sky when, coming from a house that can't be very close, he hears a lullaby, halfway between a prayer and a hopeless lament.

'We're under siege! And again today! Antiterrorist agents, soldiers from the Belgian Army, federal police! Because of the rats that have taken over the neighbourhood. The neighbourhood where my father sweated blood, and my father's father. Worked their skinny peasant backsides off. Breweries, mills, warehouses, foundries, refineries... That's what my father's father came here for! And now... we're all fucked! All terrorists! Welcome to Belgistan!'

Karolina has a very different memory of the Molenbeek Raffinerie, where she had seen dancers soar in a performance that Fenna had loved. But she doesn't say anything. She gets the feeling that just one wrong word would be enough to earn her a punch in the face or stomach. And she doesn't want to be hit any more. Not by her ex-husband, not by Andreas, not by anyone else.

She's not sure whether to carry on, and see for herself that buildings are boarded up there, where her son supposedly worked, or whether she should just go home and let that be the end of it.

Before she can even take a step, the man suddenly leaves her alone. With the bottom of his coat fluttering, he turns around, a black crow cast into the deserted streets in search of someone to bring there. Because they need to know what happened to rue de Ribaucourt ... 'Rue de Ribaucourt,' he's still repeating the words, incredulous. 'My street.' All the while shaking his head, his white hair streaked with jaundiced yellow.

13

Palermo, 29 September – 15 October

'Maybe they're aliens!' the inspector said, smiling, when the headteacher invited him to the school so that she could show him the charcoal drawings. She wanted to explain the 'hunches' that several teachers had mentioned, 'and not just them,' she added, alluding to the numerous parents who were demanding disciplinary measures. Against whom, though, no one knew.

'Hunches about what?' Inspector Vitale asked, not dropping the irony with which he had consulted the identikits, sketched with the care of someone who wanted to demonstrate their artistic talent.

'Gatherings,' said the headteacher.

'Whose gatherings?'

'During school hours,' she tried to explain, embarrassed by the condescending tone of this policeman, who had even started to look at his watch. 'At break time, or between lessons. For a while, there have been things . . .'

'Things?'

'Circumstances, events, incidents,' she corrected herself, 'which could compromise learning activities.' The technical language at least lent some formality to her words.

'So what?' the inspector asked, losing patience with this

woman, who was starting to make herself look like an annoying waste of time.

'Suspicious movements,' the headteacher came back. 'Several teachers have reported it,' she added, nodding towards the iden-tikits that the inspector had gone back to perusing half-heartedly.

'Okay,' the inspector said at last, cutting the conversation short. 'Do you want to press charges?'

'Against who?' the headteacher asked. Frankly, all she wanted was to get rid of these portraits and not have to think about them again.

Only when the inspector said the words 'persons unknown' did she relax, thinking that pressing charges against 'persons unknown', in the end, meant pressing charges against 'nobody', or rather 'nobody in particular'.

The matter would have ended there and the identikits been left to fade in another drawer, far away from the headteacher's troubled sleep, if, around a fortnight later, Inspector Vitale had not received two telephone calls, first from a colleague in Roccamena, and then directly from a senior officer in his own district.

'Off the record' was the phrase used in both cases. And the information requested concerned more or less the same thing: whether there happened to have been any reports of 'stray' minors, as his colleague from Roccamena put it.

'"Stray" in what sense?' Inspector Vitale asked, thrown by the avuncular approach. There was always a risk of confusing matters, of saying too much, when things were allowed to get informal.

'Stray ... who got away ... out of sight ... that sort of thing,' his colleague said. The inspector remembered never having thought much of him during their three years of training.

'With all these off the boats every day, I mean ...' he added, clearly alluding to the 'unaccompanied minors' who ended up who knows where, 'given that one of those *nivuru*, you know, blacks ... even turned up in the ruins of the castle'.

'What castle?'

'The Castle of Calatrasi,' his colleague said, taking the opportunity to show off his knowledge of the Arab explorer Muhammad al-Idrisi. 'And these illegals arrive by the boxful – you need a degree to figure out what kind of fish they are, and they slip in everywhere!'

With this last point, the inspector decided he'd had enough.

'Well,' is all he said, sarcastically, before ending the call with a 'Not as far as I'm concerned' so decisive that the other man didn't feel he could hold him up a minute longer.

Yet the next day, when he arrived at the office, the first thing he did was take the identikits out of his drawer and then, letting the telephone ring out, study them one by one.

Looking carefully at those faces, he noticed one particular detail that, in the end, made him call the school and ask to see the person who had drawn them.

He couldn't explain why, but the inspector liked the fact that this tiny, middle-aged woman appeared in his office one hour later, with impeccable conscientiousness, introducing herself as 'Maestra Iolanda', and that was all, except for the later addition of a surname, almost as if it were an irrelevant detail.

'Now then,' said the inspector, taking the drawings out of the plastic folder where he had kept them, which Maestra Iolanda felt showed great respect for her work.

'Yes,' she replied calmly, conscious of the great responsibility she had taken on.

'Look at this.' The inspector moved his index finger from one identikit to the next. 'Why?' he asked.

Maestra Iolanda only had to look up from the paper to give Inspector Vitale the answer to an inexplicable question. The horrified, blank-eyed expression on her face matched the one she had drawn. 'These aren't my identikits . . .' she murmured, recoiling.

'You're mistaken. They are yours. Drawn by you and given to the headteacher,' Inspector Vitale said firmly.

'But . . . they're frightening . . . those faces, I mean . . .' Maestra Iolanda said, completely bewildered, alluding to the hollow look in the children's eyes.

She couldn't go back to looking calm once she realised that the charcoal strokes really were her own.

14

Bolzano, 22 September

It had taken a long time to shake off the terror that only set in when he was already far away from that fucking-son-of-a-bitch-bastard.

The moment he'd decided to put the scissors back in his pocket, he could sense the man behind him. It's not like he actually saw him, but he got the feeling he was bearing down on him. He ran like mad.

When he managed to sneak onto the direct bus crossing the border, his legs were still shaking. The old lady sitting at the front must have realised, otherwise why would she have gently waved him over, to the seat beside her?

If it hadn't been for that old lady, he wouldn't be here, in this station nestled high in the mountains, where, any minute now, he will come out of his hiding place and launch himself into the carriage already vibrating on the platform.

He's quite sure: he only managed to cross the border because of the way the old lady reacted to the policeman who boarded the bus in the middle of the night. Khaled didn't understand what she said, but the tone was the very same one his grandmother used when she got it into her head to defend him and his brother.

'What's done is done, it's fine. They won't do it again.'

'Won't do it again my arse!' his mother would yell, holding

up the ball that had broken the umpteenth beloved vase, glass or ornament. 'And who's going to buy a new one now?' she would ask. They knew that 'who' always referred to Salim, to how much she missed him. That's why Mum got so angry, his grandmother said, because she had memories and bad thoughts. 'They'll keep doing it, you'll see ... They'll never stop.' The anger and desperation that came over her had nothing to do with the ball or the vase any more, but with *them*, the ones who took Salim, the father of her two sons, and didn't give him back.

'First choose your neighbour, then choose your house ...' his grandmother would mutter then, shaking her head and looking at the block of flats, the dirty mouths that had told who knows what lies about her son, Salim ... 'The true mosque in a pure and holy heart is builded,' she would whisper to herself. Then she would stroke both their heads. 'Let them be. They're babies.' That was how she won, on every level, because at that point his mother would drop the ball and get down on the floor to join in the cuddles around his grandmother's knees.

With the policeman, it hadn't been quite so simple – even though, a moment before he reached their row, the old lady had given Khaled a sign to pretend he was asleep, leaning on her.

The more the policeman tapped him on the shoulder to wake him up, the tighter she held him to her, protesting, raising her voice. Suddenly, a guy sitting a few seats behind stood up, furious, saying something that really upset the old lady. Khaled could feel her heart pounding under her jacket. Who knows what she must have said to that guy, and to the policeman, because some of the other passengers jumped to her defence, more women than men, while he continued to *sleep*, spark out in the arms of this old lady, who kept one hand on his forehead as if he were unwell. His mother used to do that, too, whenever he had a fever or threw up.

Between the old lady, who even started to cry, the guy who was raging against them, and the people who just wanted to get back on the road, that coach waiting at Brennero became the scene of such confusion that the policeman quickly checked the rest of the passengers and got off.

'This is how they do checks in Italy!' the guy shouted in Italian, going back to his seat.

Only the driver stayed sitting down for the whole time, his hands on the steering wheel, waiting for the scene to end.

'Next time, let's leave the *grandchildren* at home,' he said to the old lady when they reached their destination.

Khaled can still smell the old lady's perfume. That means that God exists, that he smells good, and he reveals himself to man as he sees fit, as his grandmother would have said. 'And the Devil, too,' she would have added straight after, because the Devil always came into her speeches, just like there were always 'the godless', 'the Devil's lice' who had taken Salim away, pointing a gun at his neck, when he wasn't even one of the bad guys like them. Apostasy, they said. 'Always remember, Khaled, the rope of lies is short! And even a donkey can go to Mecca, but that doesn't make him a pilgrim!' Which is how her rant would end.

The word on the display board that Khaled keeps staring at, as he waits for the right moment to hop onto the train, does look like one of the names of the cities Padre Buono had said he would pass on the journey to the south. In his vague sense of geography, this is synonymous with his vision of a land bathed by the sea, where there is none of the cold air currently chapping his face.

When he finally decides to sneak onto the train, hoping against hope that nobody stops him and his suitcase (the luggage trolley had stayed on that bastard's blue truck), a voice from across the dark platform makes him jump. So he runs. And the voice runs, too. It's following him. Even onto the train.

Now the guy is there, near him. He can feel his breath. Khaled stares straight at the ground. He doesn't even want to look, although the voice doesn't sound like it's giving orders, prohibiting, telling him to do or not do anything. It's troubled and breathless. Its tone is just asking him to look up.

Khaled doesn't understand the language, and he's so anxious, all he wants is to find a way to stash the suitcase somewhere and keep it safe, but in the end he looks up from the floor.

A man's face, Hispanic, beaten and spattered with blood, is asking him for help. As if he were a person who could help someone.

At a loss for a moment, Khaled rummages through his jacket pockets and takes out a tissue, and with the tissue, the scissors, which fall on the floor. He bends down to pick them up, but the man is gone.

Through the train window, streaked with dust and rain, he can just make him out. He's running away, terrified, flattened against a landscape of dark mountains and thorny woods that look like the very edge of the world.

15

Brussels, 22 September

And that's how Fenna had ended up throwing her out of the house. She doesn't believe it only happened because Fenna had drunk more than she had for a long time.

At seven in the evening, Karolina met her at Delirium, a pub in the middle of town, not far from the Grand Place. She hadn't been there for months, and she didn't expect it to be so crowded. Kids, mainly, sitting on stools around barrels or high tables, or in long lines at the bar.

As soon as she walked in she felt dizzy. Perhaps because of the dim yellow light in the bar. Or perhaps it was just that overwhelming feeling of very crowded spaces.

As she made her way over to the barrel where Fenna was sitting, she had the sensation that the ceiling, plastered with colourful trays showing different beer brands, was about to cave in on her with a deafening crash. Deafening, too, was the chatter around her as she stumbled towards her friend, and her loneliness, amplified by the laughter and clinking of glasses. Instinctively, as she walked through the bar she scanned faces for Andreas, even though her son had given up drinking. He'd spent his evenings shut up in his room. Playing on the computer.

That's what Karolina had told the investigators. A detail that for the Turkish officer, the one obsessed with the theory that Andreas was involved in neo-Nazi raids, was just yet another confirmation.

'Playing . . .' he'd said sarcastically, nodding. 'And at the martial arts competitions organised by Denis Nikitin, the Russian, White Rex's number one . . . no alcohol and no smoking.' He was referring to the producer of the Nazi T-shirts found among Andreas's things, at the back of the wardrobe.

Now Karolina doesn't know what to think. All she has is confusion and fear.

She'd made it, through the chaos of kegs, pressure gauges, tapping tubes, couplings, drip trays, foam scrapers, giant taps, glasses – a host of sparkling glasses hanging in racks – just so that she could talk to someone about the obsession that has been tormenting her ever since she decided to go across the canal, to Molenbeek. 'The hotbed of jihadism' they call it on the news.

Considering the anxiety that had been mounting in her body since that day, she wishes she hadn't gone at all. That's what she was thinking, as she waved to Fenna, who was calling her over.

Loneliness accompanied by an endless amount of beer. Loburg, Delirium Tremens, Delirium Nocturnum, Hy Cuvée, Leffe Blonde, American Dream.

SORRY. NO WIFI. TALK TO EACH OTHER AND GET DRUNK, a sign said. Whoever wrote it had clearly meant it to be ironic, but Karolina found it sad when she spotted it behind her friend, who had her hand up to order another round.

She wanted to tell her to stop, but she knew she'd only tell her to go to hell.

'Why?' is all she asked.

'I present: one old boot. Broke,' Fenna said, pulling out the pocket lining of the jacket she hadn't taken off, even though you could have boiled to death in there. 'Laid off, just like that.

End of story. Nothing further, your honour.' She gulped down another beer as if she was on a mission.

Meanwhile, the kids sitting nearby had a drinking style that struck Karolina as light-hearted and childlike. Just another way of having fun. She imagined what they must think, looking at them. Two overweight, middle-aged women drinking their lives away.

In the end, Karolina did drink a couple of beers herself, slowly, to fit in.

She would never have dreamed of mentioning any of her own problems that night, had Fenna not asked, 'So, what's up?' when they got to her house and she flopped down on the sofa. A gesture Karolina took as an invitation to tell all.

'Nothing,' she said at first.

'So, what's up?' Fenna said again, tensing up. 'I'm drunk. That's what you think. Well, you should know that I'm just miserable. I'm still perfectly capable. I'm not some washed-up old cow, like they think.' (*They* were the owners of the launderette. 'Restructuring and reorganising the business' was how they'd justified giving her her marching orders.)

'Like some multinational corporation . . . The Scuzzy Undies Corporation . . . So, what's up?'

Knowing how things went tonight, she can't begin to imagine how she could have considered confiding in Fenna about Andreas, the shop, the police cordons, the suspicions of 'radicalisation', the trumped-up theories of that psychologist, caseworker, plain-clothes officer, or whatever the hell she was. Definitely someone who went around wrecking other people's lives.

She even admitted Andreas's punch that broke down the door when she had asked him: 'But where do you get to all day . . . and then you're there, shut in your room . . . doing what . . .?'

'Playing. On the computer,' he'd answered, his face suddenly calm again.

She was off guard, that's it. And Fenna took advantage of that.

'You know what I say? I'm sick of your shit – you, your son, and those fanatics smashing everything up! You want to know what I think? Well, I'll tell you. Those people shut us down, take our money, throw us out into the street, they're on our back from morning to night. But them . . . they do whatever the fuck they want. *Allah akbar* and the whole country's turned upside down. They poison the air! All those rabid dogs! And your son with them . . . He's out from under your feet? It's for the best. Do you know, I'm all tangled up in here?' She jabbed her finger into her stomach. 'But I'm not ruining anyone else's life. And I don't need any help ruining my own.' She gave a sinister laugh. 'Fuck it! You'll be better off! One less piece of shit in circulation.'

Fortunately, there isn't a single beer in the house, or a drop of spirits, otherwise Karolina would have knocked back all the alcohol she hadn't drunk in her life, before she turns on the computer.

Deep in the night, sitting at Andreas's desk, she gets to thinking that the reason her son had punched down the door before he disappeared was that she was incapable of asking him the right questions.

She remembers the slip of paper she found by chance, just a few days ago, in his jeans pocket. 'Defeat is a state of mind: no one is ever defeated.' 'You must learn to live in the present and accept yourself for what you are now.' 'The end of man is action and not thought.' 'Stand not upon the order of your going. But go at once.' 'Be like water, my friend.' Underneath these quotes was a name: Bruce Lee. Karolina gave a shiver and burst into tears when she saw the words 'my friend' underlined several times, desperately.

When it comes down to it, she is someone who has never

wanted to look outside of her comfort zone. Even in the pub. The whole time, she hadn't been able to take her eyes off three girls, very young, maybe teenagers, sitting close to her and Fenna. They were also knocking back drinks as if they were on a mission, desperate to get drunk. It didn't even enter her head to ask, 'Why?'

16

Palermo, 22 October

Meanwhile, cases started to appear across the Strait of Messina.

Rumours surfaced of gangs, thugs, tiny criminals infiltrating classes. Especially in the first year of secondary school. But there, too, the 'regular' students didn't seem to have anything significant to report. No unusual violence: just punch-ups, a few attacks on pain-in-the-arse teachers, packs of boys or girls picking on someone. The few times this kind of bullying surfaced from the deathly silence of the classrooms, there were always particular names and surnames, the same down the years, with disciplinary notes in the register. And there were always parents who had to be spoken to, as if the teachers had never been kids themselves. 'Uptight', they were labelled by the spokesperson of one parents' committee in a posh neighbourhood in Naples, or perhaps Bari.

A journalist in Campania speculated on a link between these 'unexplained presences' and the report by a 'security and identity assessor' in a remote area of northern Italy, who had noticed several suspicious cases: young children, some of 'unknown origin', he said – alluding to the children of a Moroccan couple – refused to use their badges to clock in and out of school. 'Using them teaches young people to respect the institutions of our country.'

So, the case landed straight on the desk at the police station, and was, in turn, passed on to the chief.

'Typical police,' scoffed the senior editor of one of Sicily's top newspapers when he heard that the story of the 'illegals' had even reached the interregional headquarters of the carabinieri in Sicily and Calabria. That was also a rumour. No confirmation and no denial.

What definitely did happen concerned a couple of decisions that Inspector Vitale had made after witnessing the terror in Maestra Iolanda's eyes.

'Our job is to make people feel safe, to dispel fear, regardless of any danger. If it doesn't exist, we'll deal with it all the same. That's what it means to be on the force.' Inspector Vitale had never forgotten these words. He couldn't remember exactly where he'd heard them, or who from, whether it was in real life or in a film, but when he'd signed up, it had been because of the dignity that, as a boy, he'd attributed to this way of 'serving'. So, in spite of the banality of his everyday 'service', he'd never broken the promise he'd made to himself in those years when the only other job he could imagine doing was being a fireman. Those big childhood decisions.

Even though he wasn't entirely sure it was the right thing, he sent a unit to patrol the neighbourhood.

Getting the identikits distributed around Maestra Iolanda's school was slightly more complicated, but in the end, Inspector Vitale found a solution he thought would spare him any complaints or reports of having caused alarm.

Officially, the meticulous work was the result of the initiative of an unknown group. Someone even labelled them 'hard-working custodians of security' – do-gooders, in other words.

In the space of one night, a fair number of lamp posts, tree trunks, post boxes and advertising hoardings were pasted with charcoal sketches of children's faces with the message: IF YOU HAVE ANY INFORMATION, PLEASE CONTACT THE AREA COMMAND.

The effect of this thorough posting job was that, walking around the local streets, turning a corner and especially sitting on a bench in the well-lit, tree-lined square, people found themselves suddenly plunged into a landscape of brown faces with wild eyes repeated ad infinitum, wherever they looked.

Even Inspector Vitale was forced to disapprove of the dedication his men had shown to the task, which was perhaps due to the fact that their own kids went to the school where there were rumours of children at risk of flying out of the windows and cracking their faces open, or flying up into the classrooms, illegally.

As he paced the streets, he couldn't help but feel uneasy in front of the eyes staring out at the entire neighbourhood and which, when so wantonly replicated, seemed to belong to creatures that were even more distressed.

'What a ridiculous idea! And the consequences ...' the head-teacher yelled, turning pale and summoning Maestra Iolanda immediately.

17

Northern Italy,
22 September – 22 October

He got on and off buses and trains at stations and stops he didn't even know the names of. He covered long distances on foot without knowing where the city ended – past shopping centres, car parks with sparkling windscreens, railways – and where the countryside began: cultivated fields and farmhouses in a rust-yellow landscape that smelled like rain, even when it hadn't been raining. If he had to say what he would really have liked to show Nadir, he knew what he'd pick: the morning fog that smoked across the fields, like steam from a giant pot.

He even managed to ride a few stops on a school bus for visually impaired kids. One of them even asked him to help unfasten their jacket because the zip was stuck, and when one of the girls sitting behind Khaled said, 'You stink. Oh, you're mute! You stink, you know?' the same boy shut her up with a whole argument about the ventilation system on the bus, which was a real piece of junk. 'Don't worry, brother,' he confided. 'Washing's a real effort for me, too.'

After the ordeal with the lorry driver, he steered clear of hitch-hiking. But a couple of times, he managed to climb onto the back bumper of a lorry, miraculously pulling the suitcase behind him with a strength he didn't know he had. Gripping the tailboard, he chewed through mouthfuls of dust and smoke.

When he set off on the road weeks ago, he couldn't have imagined all this crazy roving around. He was sure that the south was at the end of one long, straight road, but maybe he hadn't understood Padre Buono's directions properly. This hadn't been in the plan before Nadir died the way he died, because of some fucked-up thing that would never have happened if he'd done his job as a big brother.

In the end, he stopped in a city by a river. Padre Buono had spelled out its name several times: To-ri-no. Turin. 'There are friends there who can help you out.'

When he reached the enormous disused factory where they 'resided' (that was Padre Buono's word), there was no one inside, except for an old man.

There must have been a whole load of people here until a few days ago, judging from the number of blankets, clothes, mattresses and rags clustered in certain areas of the warehouse. Bottles and stacks of crushed cans were scattered all over, especially in the yard, among tangles of brushwood, on top of bits of brick and dust.

'Careful.' That's how the old man introduced himself.

The fact that Khaled understood every word spoken by this big, tall man – or maybe the coat just made him look imposing – suddenly made him feel better, even though he was exhausted. He'd never thought about his own language like that: like a warm bath he could slip into, offering a bit of comfort.

In the days he spent at the dilapidated old factory, the one thing that never left him was the nausea. Because of the stench, a concentrate of faeces, urine, food, alcohol and embers – a kind of bubble that intensified even more when the old man heated up 'stuff to eat' on a camping stove, the most precious thing he owned, along with his knife.

'At the back there, Central Africans. On the right, Romanians; there, North Africans, and fucked right off over there, the junkies.' Now they'd all packed up and gone. But the old man never explained why. He just showed Khaled the little room where his bed was: a mattress on a wooden table and, beside it, a stub of a candle. He was particularly proud of the bars on the large window through which the light fell directly onto the bed. 'First-rate work,' he said, pointing at it like someone who knows what they're talking about. 'And this old carcass,' he added, digging his fat, wonky thumb into his chest, 'isn't going anywhere, not even if they come in here with bombs.'

Khaled screamed like crazy when he heard the crash. The commotion had jolted him out of a deep sleep. At first he lay petrified, his face pressed into the mattress, with the deafening sound of caterpillar tracks crushing iron and stone in the middle of the yard. Then he jumped up.

With slow, dinosaur-like movements and huge pincers, the machine broke and mangled sheet metal and frames as if they were as soft as butter.

It was on the second roar, as a dust cloud invaded the warehouse, that Khaled darted into the old man's room. He shrieked that there was a war outside. But nothing. The man raised one arm and then gave a sign with his enormous wonky thumb as if to say, 'It's all okay,' just as a piece of metal and a shower of glass crashed to the floor nearby. Then, Khaled started to tug at the old man's arm, in an attempt to drag him out of the room. At that very moment, the glass in the large window, and the bars with it, literally exploded onto the bed.

He can't remember how he ended up face-down on the floor. He only remembers that, when he managed to get to his feet, spluttering in the middle of a greasy cloud that made it difficult to breathe, he could see the body bundled up in the coat, in among the rubble. The old man's face and hair white with a powder that didn't look real, and in the middle of his forehead, a red trickle of blood. It ran onto his nose, between his unblinking eyes fixed on the filthy patch of sky the machine had opened above his head.

'Stupid old man!' Khaled yelled, hunting for the suitcase in the wreckage, swearing and almost crying in the effort to pull it out from under a girder, grazing his hands and knees, and finally running as far away as possible. 'Stupid old man!' he kept saying to himself, with a lump in his throat, as if he had to stay there with that guy for the rest of his life. He was a moron, that's what he was!

Crouching by the river that runs through the middle of the city Khaled is about to leave, he thinks back to something the old man had told him one night, spurred on by wine and the crackling of a fire he'd made like a work of art.

He'd gestured to the iron structure holding up the vast warehouse. 'Imagine how it must have been ... building engines for boats ... huge beautiful machines ...' Even he, who had been a metalworker in his country, had trouble imagining it. 'Engines. For. Boats,' he repeated, enunciating slowly, full of admiration. 'It's beautiful, sailing,' he said at last, evoking something immeasurable. And then, poking his arthritic finger into Khaled's chest, he breathed into his face the booze-soaked phrase: 'When you have a destination, even the desert becomes a road.'

Crouching by the river, Khaled wraps his arms around the suitcase standing on its wheels. Tomorrow he will resume his journey. He has a whole night to contemplate the duplication of trees and lights on the dark, glossy surface of the water. And its gentle yellow-brown shimmer, a liquid stillness he had never imagined, offers some consolation as he strokes the salvaged red plastic suitcase.

18

Brussels, 22 September – 22 October

She hates herself, despises herself. Yet, as soon as she finishes work, the only purpose to her day is to go home and sit at the computer, which she leaves permanently switched on. She thought she might find it comforting, but instead she goes from a hypnotic trance to dismay as she spends hours watching crazy videos.

At first, she'd concentrated on the files saved on the desktop. The background is a sunset, but sinister. A yellow sun looming over a tundra of earthy islands.

NSU. Underground guerillas, the title of one file last edited by Andreas a couple of years ago. Inside, notes about the kids from Winzerla in Jena in the nineties, and the attacks between 2000 and 2011. Hamburg, Munich, Rostock, Cologne, Dortmund, Kassel, Nuremberg. '*Döner-Morde*', Kebab Murders, the press called them. In particular, a file containing a list of crimes committed by one of them, Uwe Mundlos.

Uwe Mundlos, the angel-faced German who, as a boy, created an antisemitic video game with the march of the Third Reich as its soundtrack. Uwe Mundlos, who walked around in broad daylight in Winzerla, his district of Jena, dressed in an SS uniform. Uwe Mundlos who, with his friends Uwe Böhnhardt and Beate Zschäpe, secretly committed crimes: robberies, bombings, executions of *Kanaken*, people from Turkey and the Middle East. 'Suitcases full of explosives ... boom. Torch + explosives June 1999, Nuremberg ... boom. Bomb with 5.5 kilos of TNT and nails, June 2004, Cologne ... Boom boom boom!' Andreas had noted, along with a reminder: 'Read: Hans von Dach, *Total Resistance. The ABC of guerrilla warfare.*' Uwe Mundlos, who supported his life in hiding by selling a neo-Nazi version of Monopoly: Pogromly. Uwe Mundlos, who contributed to designing a Bart Simpson 'Skinson' cartoon to be printed on T-shirts. Uwe Mundlos and Uwe Böhnhardt who, on 4 November 2011 in Eisenach, shot each other in a caravan to avoid being caught by the police. And the band Gigi & Die Braunen Stadtmusikanten, who wrote a song dedicated to the *Döner-Morde* on their CD: *Adolf Hitler lebt!*

In another folder, Karolina found photos. Photos of Andreas posing with his friends after a kickboxing match: holding his mouthguard up to the lens, or grappling in the ring. On his back was a tattoo of a snake that she had no idea about, in fact she's sure he must not have had it the last time she saw him with his shoulders bare. MIXED MARTIAL ARTS CHAMPIONSHIP. SPECIALISATION: GROUND & POUND, it was titled.

In another folder, the recurring name among strings of websites and URLs for YouTube channels was Denis Nikitin. Nikitin, the Russian with his 'Zero Tolerance' sweatshirts and T-shirts, accessories with the Black Suns the Turkish police officer had shown her. Nikitin and the White Rex doctrine: revive the spirit of the fighter, the warriors; remember our glorious ancestors, the Vikings, the Praetorian Guard, the Crusaders ... Glory and honour. Nikitin, who organises events throughout Europe, Belgium, Germany, Russia, Italy, France, Switzerland, Greece, mixed marital arts tournaments and cage fighting. WHITE REX – WARRIOR SPIRIT. WHITE POWER, it was titled. Nikitin, who promotes black metal concerts.

Gripped by a sort of euphoria, Karolina even thought of calling Fenna to tell her that her son had nothing to do with anyone from the 'hotbed' of Molenbeek, the Sharia4Belgium fanatics, the *allah akbar*. That life-wrecking psychologist was completely wrong!

The last folder, created and edited by Andreas a few months before he disappeared, contains a single file with the name *Deso Dogg*.

Who Deso Dogg was, Karolina discovered by browsing rap videos, clips of martial arts matches and YouTube channels of jihadist propaganda, which turned her world and her thoughts upside down all over again.

That was when she decided to go to the gym Andreas had been using.

The entrance to the basement has MMA FIGHTER written across it. It's in a neighbourhood whose residents do nothing but sleep there and leave. Through the iron door, though, the atmosphere is comfortable, illuminated by LEDs that simulate daylight. She likes walking on the linoleum that smells brand new.

There is no one at the reception desk. So Karolina follows the syncopated voices coming from the hall. Gathered around a tatami, several boys are studying the moves of athletes who size each other up and then grab hold, landing entwined on the mat, while the younger ones, ten or twelve years old, try out punches on a mat nearby; they are all focused, under the watchful gaze of someone who seems to be the teacher. Standing with his arms folded, in a shirt so wide there is only a hint of the muscles beneath, he follows their every move. From time to time, he adjusts their posture. 'No blind moves. Self-control and slow movements,' he explains.

The vast turquoise walls are calming, even though there is a palpable sense of the force of the bodies on the tatami, the tension escaping in sudden cries, breaking the constant hum of the ventilation fans.

No one seems to notice the figure bundled up in a cream coat that must make her look even more pudgy and awkward. Just one boy in a ripped tracksuit and baggy T-shirt comes over to her.

'Can I help you?' he asks, politely. In that moment, Karolina realises something that troubles her. If she'd met these boys in the street, in gangs of three or four, she would have given them a wide berth.

When she finds herself face-to-face with the teacher, sitting at a desk in a small office with a window onto the training hall, she feels a surge of pride, and even gratitude, to hear that Andreas was a quiet type who kept his head down and got on with his training. 'They're usually the best ones.' No one has ever said anything like that about her son. 'His only flaw was that his tracksuits were too fancy, too showy.'

'He liked to dress well,' Karolina wants to explain, but the teacher doesn't seem to appreciate any conversation that doesn't directly relate to his discipline, as if the meaning of his work is all there is.

Apart from that, she doesn't manage to find out much about Andreas's life; whether, for example, he'd made any friends there. But she does manage to bring the conversation round to the topic of Deso Dogg . . .

'You really want to know what I think of him? An elusive German rapper and fighter, who ended up where he did, in Syria, fighting . . .' the teacher says, his voice quiet but his face tense. 'Well, personally, I think he's a failed rapper, a failed fighter, a failed Muslim.' Then he pats his chest. 'I am also a fighter, a warrior and a Muslim, for what it's worth, and . . . what I'm trying to teach my boys, partly, I learned from the Koran. From the Koran, not from YouTube.' He stops short, with such contempt that she feels humiliated. 'If your son thinks Deso Dogg is the best . . . then he did the right thing not coming back to my gym. Good evening.' He reaches out for a handshake that is in no way hostile. If anything it seems to encourage her not to give in to the ghosts.

The ghosts that have haunted her thoughts since she started browsing websites, blogs, YouTube channels, flipping from one extreme to the other . . . and which, as Karolina makes her way home on the metro, in the drone of the carriage, condense into one jumble of voices, as if all the videos she's seen, and the phrases she's read, all the delirious arguments, the calls, the statements, the threats, were now poking fun at her, at her pain.

'We, the Aryan minority, universally despised and ridiculed in Europe, are fighting for a new world order: one nation for every population! – If you reject the system, they arrest you, they take your money, persecute your family. But Islam will conquer the world, my brothers! – We have to free Belgium from rapist immigrants! – Free Belgium from injustice, guarantee the safety of Belgian Muslims! – Free Belgium from the illegals! – Free Belgium from the idolatry of apostates! – Modern society breeds philistines and consumers. We want warriors! – We have to fight the evils of Taghut, rebel, reject idols and false gods, my brothers! – Against capitalism, Europe, immigrants! – Communism is dead, capitalism is dying, Islam is rebirth! – No alcohol, no gambling, no drugs, comrades! – We want people who are physically and morally strong, Muslim brothers. No alcohol, no smoking! – It's only a matter of time, Muslim brothers. There's no problem. We will have no problem! – It's only a matter of time, comrades! – Democracy is hypocrisy, Muslim brothers! – Democracy is hypocrisy, comrades!'

This jumble of frighteningly similar jihadi and neo-Nazi proclamations brought her to the verge of tears. She thinks back to the cleanliness and order of the gym, how through the teacher's methods they became actions, words. Quite the opposite of the mess she's stumbling around in.

'Where did you end up?' she whispers, crying dry tears that hurt all the more.

19

Palermo, 22–30 October

Maestra Iolanda stood for minutes by the desk, her eyes welling up. She didn't want to sit down, thank you. Inspector Vitale gave her a disheartened look. They had reached 'contagion'. Her sketches had gone viral on the internet. It was impossible to trace the first person who had posted on Facebook, Twitter, Instagram, Tumblr, or Google Plus about the identikits pasted around the neighbourhood, on trees and lamp posts. Some people thought it had all started as a WhatsApp message sent as a joke.

The first consequence had been a written warning from the headteacher, as if she wasn't the person who'd given the sketches to the police. Now, Maestra Iolanda was afraid not only of being reported, but of a suspension for 'actions not in keeping with the responsibility, duties and integrity essential to the role'. Just the wording of those accusations knocked her sideways.

She wasn't explicitly asking for the inspector's help. She just wanted to let him know. Nor did she want to accuse him of anything in particular. She had drawn the sketches with her own hands, and, with her own hands, she had given them to the headteacher. She wasn't one to shirk her responsibilities. But . . . She couldn't believe that things were getting out of hand like this and it was all on her shoulders.

With this last point, she started to cry, tears streaming silently down her face. She would have taken out a handkerchief, but she was too embarrassed. She wasn't used to public displays of emotion.

Inspector Vitale had been having his own problems for a few days now. The more the identikits passed from profile to profile and from one social network to another, the higher the number of reports of 'illegal' children and complaints against unknowns, accompanied by a multitude of bad photographs taken on mobile phones: wiry figures curled up, perched, always shadowy, elusive and, in a couple of cases, caught in freefall, like stones from the sky.

At first, the reports and complaints came straight to his station, since that was the 'identikit district'. But when the news came out about the tracks in the sand that prompted the beach cleaner to whisper, 'Rats!' on the morning of 11 September ('Over a month ago!' someone railed on the pages of an angry blog), when it became clear that this story had been going on for who knows how long, the case spread like wildfire, involving specialised units, territorial commands, regional commands – even the interregional command had, begrudgingly, called him to find out the substance of this threat, or rather, this 'poppycock'.

The first media outlet that gave any serious consideration to the fears that were now snaking around provinces in the north of the country was a local television station in Veneto. Later, someone would credit a station in Lombardy with making the first broadcast about what would soon be uncompromisingly described as 'an enigma on a global scale'.

'Social alarm' was the term chosen by newsrooms to launch the story of a case that would only add to older kinds of alarm and fear at the root of tensions that had gone dangerously ignored. Like the story of the bruises.

'What bruises?' the programme's director asked.

'Swelling and bruises of unknown origin that appeared on the arms of several children – not one or two, you know, quite a number! Just like that – when they came out of school.'

Where this happened was not entirely clear to the journalist, who vaguely referenced San Zenone, without specifying which one (San Zenone al Lambro in Milan, San Zenone al Po in Pavia, or San Zenone degli Ezzelini in Treviso).

He didn't mention that an entomologist had posited the hypothesis that the bruises were a result of bites from the tiger mosquito, a black, hairy and particularly aggressive variety that was rife thanks to the unusual temperatures recorded across the continent in the middle of the Mediterranean anticyclone.

'The problem is not whether these *illegals* are *literally* going in and out of classrooms, sticking needles or spikes into children's arms,' argued the journalist, who was set on running this story. 'It's a question of points of view. And my point of view is *they might not even exist* – I admit, there's no evidence – but *people's fear does exist*. And *that* is what I have a duty to report on,' he concluded in a grave tone that had considerable bearing on the director's decision.

The fear he referred to concerned a municipality on the border of Veneto and Lombardy.

A retired teacher who had a long history of participation in the local neighbourhood watch tried to collar a couple of these kids outside different schools. But no luck. 'They slipped through my fingers! Li-te-ra-lly, God knows …' he babbled, without managing to explain exactly what had happened. He said it again and again, staring into space, as though the kids were right there, mocking him.

A group of parents, huddled around the former teacher, said they were sure that these were the same kids whose photos had been circulating on the internet for days. (Nobody said it would be more appropriate to call them charcoal drawings.) The very identikits that meant that Maestra Iolanda, at the other end of the country, couldn't sleep a wink at night. An insignificant creature! She repeated this, inspecting the dark circles under her eyes in the mirror, in the dim glow of an energy-saving light bulb, to distance herself from the idea that, in the end, it would be her head that rolled.

Since it wasn't entirely clear what kind of individuals should be watched, stopped or turned in to the police, plenty of local administrations encouraged the creation of special patrols against the 'illegals' swarming up 'to our north from the furthest coasts in the south'. One mayor in Pavia didn't mince his words: 'We should dress them up as rabbits and go bam bam bam with a shotgun,' he said with a laugh, winning support from his electorate.

That this was the way the phenomenon was spreading was soon confirmed by an otherwise inexplicable and chilling event that Inspector Vitale would have preferred to keep to himself, had someone not thought to feed it to the press – probably one of his men, who probably took offence at being called 'irresponsible'. That was the word Inspector Vitale used to describe the stupidity of distributing Maestra Iolanda's identikits in such a mindless, idiotic way, even though it was clear that what he was really thinking was, 'You bunch of pricks!' So, someone took offence and channelled it into a news leak.

THE MYSTERY OF THE LIVE CHILDREN. With that headline, the Palermo edition of one of the national papers informed its readers of what had happened a couple of days earlier at the police station. An unfortunate, humiliating and vaguely gruesome situation, which Inspector Vitale would never have wanted to read about when he opened the newspaper on the morning of

30 October. In fact, after a quick glance at the first few lines – complete with photos of himself and of Corporal Genovesi, taken in secret, a dazed expression on his face – he closed the paper and waited for the inevitable to happen. It materialised just a few hours later, in the form of an urgent and entirely unusual call that made him jump out of his seat, launching him headlong into the struggle to find the right words to explain to the defence chief, 'You really had to be there to . . .'

That was the only coherent sentence, even though it was unfinished, that Inspector Vitale managed to say about what happened – on 28 October, yes; at the police station under his command, yes.

The rest was a crackpot theory that he could hardly believe himself.

20

Textile district of Prato, 22–30 October

If Khaled had known what was happening all across the country, and in particular what was about to happen in the Po valley, he probably would have stayed there, covering his tracks between the ghost factories on the outskirts of a city he would never know the name of, much less whether there was a river running through the middle of it.

It was the old man who put him in touch with the guy who had to take a shipment of goods to south-central Italy. Fortunately that happened a couple of days before the digger's jaws bit into the roof, before the shock, the roar and the final glimpse of the sky for the old man who, in the end, didn't give a shit about anything, including him. It was a good job that the night he'd drunkenly slurred, 'What have you got in there?', pointing his arthritic thumb at the suitcase, Khaled had managed to keep his mouth shut. The old man didn't deserve to know his business. He thinks this sitting in the van beside a guy with an Asian face and shaggy hair, who would look like a child but for the fine lines on his cheeks and forehead. He even has small, slender hands. Khaled notices them when the man hands him a parcel with food inside, something sweet and sour that he sort of likes and sort of doesn't. But he eats it and that's enough.

This boyish Asian guy had picked him up at dawn not far from the riverbank where Khaled spent the night, his last in the 'city of glass mountains', as he now calls it. When he woke up, in the grey morning, in the distance he could see a crown of bright white peaks, shining like glass scales, like the backbone of a dinosaur whose tail, he imagined, was the river that stretched out, still and long, before his eyes.

Since he got into the van, this is the first gesture the Asian man has bothered to make towards him, focused as he is on driving and the cameras caught by the beep of a device fixed to the windscreen. Every time he hears it, he turns to look at the side of the road, as if to check that there isn't a roadblock or anyone he doesn't want to meet. You can tell from the way his forehead wrinkles.

At one point, Khaled finally catches sight of the sea. That means he knows he's going in the right direction. The old man had been honest with him, he has to give him that. He'd set him back on the path he had lost. 'When you have a destination, even the desert becomes a road,' he says to himself, recalling the old man's words. His way of saying thank you.

This is the spirit in which he approaches the last leg of the journey, even when the sea disappears from view. 'It'll be back,' he thinks, as the van makes its way through fields and turns onto a main road. Tower blocks and factories. Or rather tower blocks that look like factories where, through the windows, you can make out machinery in crowded rooms; and warehouses with window bars that sometimes allow a glimpse of a real life. It reminds Khaled of his mother's laundry and the simple kitchen where she would prepare dinner, even if as time went on there had been less and less food to cook, or maybe she just hadn't felt like cooking any more.

He's not sure whether these memories can be considered some

of the 'nice things' he's nostalgic for, or whether this is plunging
him further into the sadness that used to come over him in the
hut at dawn, when he would open his eyes to the sound of the
padlock and chain banging on the door as Padre Buono said,
'Here's the bread and here's the milk.' He would have to shake
Nadir and bring him the bowl so he could pee, being careful
not to tread in the gross black goo spread all over the floor to
catch the cockroaches from the bits of food left over from the day
before. At night he was so dead tired, he left the food that Nadir
hadn't finished next to the mattress. 'The best way to fatten up
the cockroaches,' Padre Buono would say, angry. Because of
people like him, who couldn't be arsed to put the rubbish in the
buckets, he had to buy all that goo every month, 'to keep the
place clean'. Even though the bottom of the slop buckets was
where the cockroaches made their nests to lay their black eggs.

That there is nothing for him to do but mind his own business for half an hour or so, he understands from the gesture the
man used to encourage him to take a walk, as the iron door slid
shut, and another Asian man – who looks to Khaled, like the
twin brother of the one who'd brought him there – drives up to
the van with a forklift full of packaged stuff. Others, cousins or
more twins, move quickly in the semi-darkness of a place that
seems huge, hoisting enormous packages on pallets. Frenetic
and precise work carried out in the kind of silence that reminds
Khaled of those very old films his grandmother, Samira, loved.
As if they can't speak. 'You're all so good at talking. What about
working?' Padre Buono would always say. A team of mutes
chosen specially for this job.

The road Khaled takes while he waits for the loading opera-
tion to finish gives him the feeling of walking through a hall of
mirrors: signs, all the same, painted in a whirl of reds, yellows,
oranges and blues that leave him dazed. Khaled can guess what

kind of business is being done, but he wouldn't be able to tell anyone where to come in, exactly, or what to buy.

A place designed to make him get lost again and never come out!

The stress pumps through his head. He looks for the road he came down, cursing this silent way of working that means he can't follow the sound of voices, between tower blocks that look like miniature factories and warehouses that seem like enormous, overcrowded homes.

If Khaled had known what was going on all across the country, and in particular what was about to happen nearby, he wouldn't have cared about the fact that, when he finally gets back on the right street, the area in front of the warehouse is empty, as if there had never been any frantic toing and froing by the cousins and twins. The guy is ready to set off again, without giving a shit about Khaled. He had almost left him there.

If Khaled had known, he would have changed his plans and headed over the Apennines towards the valley, forgetting about the shining mountains, the magic dinosaur, its tail in the shape of a river . . . and the sea. Maybe he would even have ditched the red suitcase, if only he'd known.

21

Brussels, 22–30 October

For a few days Karolina has been carefully listening to all the news she can, scouring images, her eyes burning from the hours spent in front of the computer. She doesn't follow any particular criteria; she watches everything and listens hungrily: if a drug gang gets taken down in a nearby neighbourhood; if there's news of a gunfight, movements of armed groups or bombings in territories she knows nothing about; if they catch some new presumed terrorist; if they talk about dogs rescued from an underground fighting ring, since Andreas always loved dogs (he'd come to blows with a 'lowlife' once, defending a 'little creature' that was being kicked). Even when there are features on volunteers going to help out in some disaster-struck part of the world, she's there, waiting, all ears.

Her son could be anywhere, at the end of the day, doing anything. He could also simply have disappeared, decided to vanish without a trace. And that's his right, too. For her, this is a way to console herself, or at least not to lose hope.

The one thing Karolina can't bring herself to think is that Andreas could be dead. That's what makes her so sure that, sooner or later, she will do it: if not find him, at least see him or catch a glimpse of him, if only for a split second on the television or internet, with all these videos people post every day from all over the world. Or, maybe, she could dream about him. Even a nightmare would do. But when it comes to hearing his voice, Karolina has given up hope, exhausted from waiting. She'd even sewn herself a little pouch to tie onto her belt, so she could keep her phone close, literally on the hip where she'd held Andreas as a baby with his legs around her body.

This is why, the night before she decided to go back over the Charleroi canal so that she could properly see rue de Ribaucourt sealed off, it seems only natural – considering the amount of news she's been watching and listening to for a while – that she would notice a sudden shift in how the news was being presented.

'Terror alerts' had almost vanished from more than one news programme. They'd started talking, above all and with particular insistence, about the new waves of migrants arriving along the Mediterranean route. Even though the most recent statistics would suggest that displaced people had actually been concentrating on the Balkan route for some time now. 'Unaccompanied minors' was the mantra repeated by several broadcasters, along with another story immediately afterwards: the need to adopt new security measures in the country's schools, as had already happened elsewhere in Europe. On the radio it was the same thing. Even the updates on her phone followed the same pattern.

Karolina kept mulling this over, even during the lonely hours in the deserted, geometric spaces of the estate agency, as she polished desks and did the hoovering. It was a way of distracting herself, perhaps, of keeping her brain focused on something other than her son.

Once she is on the metro to the canal, though, it is out of her thoughts. Her mind is busy going over the route she plans to take, more or less the same as a month ago: quai des

Charbonnages, rue de la Prospérité, place Saint-Jean Baptiste, rue du Comte de Flandre, Gemeenteplaats, and then back again, towards rue de Ribaucourt.

Only today it is very cold and rainy. She hates the relentless veil of fat little droplets, like a spray that never stops and, with the lashing wind, creeps into everywhere, not giving a damn about umbrellas, raincoats, anoraks, or her jacket that is in no way fit to keep her dry.

She isn't prepared for the surprise that greets her when she arrives in Molenbeek. And not because the streets are deserted and fearful. As soon as she turns out of rue de la Prospérité, which is always bare and sad, she finds herself in a bustle of people coming and going from grocers, fishmongers, butchers' shops. The hubbub becomes a crowd and a jungle of umbrellas when Karolina reaches the market in the square, Gemeenteplaats, between stalls laden with fruit and vegetables, bulging carrier bags, shopping trolleys squashing people's toes, and shreds of paper stuck to the pavement.

Even the narrow rue du Prado is brimming and swaying. Karolina stops to look at the square: a whole street full of goods sheltered by sheets of cling film streaked with rain, and in the middle, a stream of people busy haggling, buying, moving peacefully from one shop to the next. As if this place were no longer the 'hotbed', 'Belgistan', monitored by the army, under special surveillance and out of bounds – the poisoned belly of the nation and of all of Europe. As if she hadn't been there just a few weeks ago, a month at most, and hadn't seen with her own eyes the fear filtering through the walls, the red bricks of the tower blocks, the blacked-out windows and the face of the old man with the jaundiced hair, who went to and fro, bringing people to see for themselves.

She looks around, expecting to spot an armoured vehicle, a patrol from the local police, the federal police, or at least the face of that particular breed of psychologist or special forces agent who came right into her house to tell her about Andreas, the cordons, the terrorists of Ribaucourt. A sign, that's what she wants, a sign that gives her a single *rational reason* for being there, looking for a trace of her son.

She's struck by the wail of a child staring at her from a pram. A gunshot that brings her to her senses. Only now does she realise what she's doing. Standing between the square and the entrance to rue du Prado, for several minutes she's been gazing at the women walking by in niqabs, trying to examine their eyes through the slit in their headscarves. She couldn't say whether it's because of all that black they're swathed in, or because of the silent and unexpected fluttering of their dresses a whisper away from her, the fact is, she's staring at them, one after the other, watching for any possible hidden gestures under the niqab. There is only one thought on her mind: getting her son out of there, freeing him from that tomb.

'I'm going mad,' she says, dripping with rain, when she finds herself calling her ex-husband, who responds with a long silence.
    'I'm telling you, I'm going mad . . .'
    'Go mad on your own. As far as I'm concerned . . . him . . . he's gone, finished. Dead.'
    'There's no trace of anything left. Why is there no trace of anything left?' she insists, desperately, referring to the 'hotbed', the boarded-up shop where her son had supposedly worked, the state of alert, the stories that have vanished from the news, as if not only the news, but also Andreas, and all hope, has been lost.
    'The psychologist, that woman, she said that's where he'd

ended up . . . and now there's nothing left, nothing at all, do you see?' she finally mumbles.

'Yes, you are going mad,' is the only response she gets, a moment before the line goes completely silent.

22

Brussels, Rome, Palermo, 31 October

The superintendent of the Brussels West Police Department, the Italian defence chief, and Inspector Vitale, at the police station where it all began, thought they were going mad that night, not even forty-eight hours after Karolina had found herself searching for her son under the niqabs of women in the street.

All three were sitting on the sofa in their own living rooms, miles away from one another, quietly watching the news. None of them had drunk any more than usual. One glass of wine or a beer, two at most. Only the Belgian police superintendent had eaten anything remotely heavy: a large portion of *boulettes* with sauce. All in all, nothing out of the ordinary.

Although they were on different channels, and in different countries – at least the Belgian broadcaster was – in all three cases, the news report was about the unusual weather conditions across the continent: consistently sunny, thanks to a large anticyclone set to settle over Europe again in the next few days; temperatures above the seasonal average; higher pressure; calm winds and seas. A few more days of glorious weather then, followed immediately by thunderstorms in the north, and increasingly unstable conditions across the rest of the continent.

The air force colonel who Inspector Vitale was listening to had just come out with a phrase that concerned him: 'From tomorrow, flat calm between the Strait of Sicily and Malta Channel.'

It was not that the inspector preferred bad weather, but he got the feeling that there was an allusion in those words, almost a veiled hint of new boats arriving from the North African coast. That was how it had happened in September, anyway. The hardest month the coastguard had faced in all these years of shipwrecks, search and rescue. The thing Inspector Vitale had been most afraid of for some time around there. Especially after the shambles at the police station on 28 October that had meant he had to face yesterday's embarrassing phone call with none other than the defence chief.

This was why, as soon as he heard those words, he kicked the footstool out from under his feet and went to stand up, determined to silence the colonel and his forecasts with a swift click of the remote.

No such stress affected the mood of the superintendent of the Brussels West Police Department, or the Italian defence chief. They were caught by surprise in the flat calm of their living rooms at the moment when they were at their most defenceless: when they were thinking that the day had nothing else in store for them. Maybe that even contributed to how slowly they reacted, powerless in the face of the unexpected.

In the bluish glow from the screen, all three got the impression, and quickly became sure, that there was someone sitting, in fact perched, on top of their television set. That this was no hallucination became clear when they decided to switch on the light and, looking back, saw two skinny legs dangling in front of the screen. Even the feet were skinny and bare, much more real than the advert that had suddenly pushed up the volume on the TV. Concentrating on this weird creature, the two senior officials didn't even try to turn off the television. Only Inspector

Vitale did, in his attempt to get rid of the figure before him, to vaporise it in the darkness of the screen.

The superintendent of the Brussels West Police Department, who was otherwise a very practical man, took his time to compose what he felt was a sensible thought, in the face of such nonsense: if this child were really there, in the living room in his house, he would simply need to go up to the television, taking care not to let him get away, and pull him down by the arm, scrawny little thing that he was. The rest he could decide later. It was just that, as soon as he tried to take a step, he was seized by a fear he couldn't explain. Not because the child had moved, pulled out a knife, or a gun. He hadn't moved a millimetre. What was paralysing the superintendent was the way the child so intently watched him walk towards him. And the eyes. Unmoving and dark, as dark as the depths of the sea. He couldn't imagine, in that moment, that he would spend an entire night like that, standing in front of the television, staring at a child who was staring right back at him.

The Italian defence chief also spent all night on his feet, wondering whether Inspector Vitale had felt the same sense of inevitability when he found himself caught up in the story of the 'live children'. He stared into the deep ocean of those pupils and the more he was compelled to keep looking straight ahead, the more he grasped precisely what Inspector Vitale had meant when he said that 'You really had to be there' to understand what had happened at the police station in Palermo.

The commotion Inspector Vitale had happened to 'be there' for didn't protect him from the shock. The face of the little boy perched on top of the television bore a surprising resemblance to the outline of one of the identikits drawn by Maestra Iolanda.

Frozen in front of the screen, certain that the child wasn't really there, in his own home, before his eyes, he tried to reconstruct, as accurately as he could, how things had gone on the morning of 28 October, regardless of the fact that he had promised himself he wouldn't go over it again, determined that the story of the 'live children' would remain, at least as far as he was concerned, a sensationalist gimmick concocted by a newspaper to help them deal with the crisis in print news.

It had been a slightly cloudy late-October day. As with every morning, the cleaning lady had made him coffee that tasted burnt. A simple question of proportion, which she absolutely refused to contemplate: more water or less grounds. Her usual conclusion: 'Why don't you just buy a coffee machine that does everything for you?' Inspector Vitale had become accustomed to this daily argument. 'Because I like the smell,' he had been replying for years.

Apart from not being able to get the unpleasant taste out of his mouth (despite drinking three insipid coffees from the machine at the station, which gave off the same smell of warm water with every drink it released), and apart from a few problems he'd resolved by making some calls, after a difficult week spent trying to play down the business with the identikits – at least in public – the only thought really occupying his mind, until mid-morning that day, was whether it was appropriate to ask the waitress from the bar opposite the office out to dinner. She was a vivacious woman who made people happy, which was the thing he needed the most: a bit of carefree fun that might last until the morning.

The first sign of what would happen a couple of hours later was unique, not to say bizarre. Various foreigners started arriving at the police station in dribs and drabs, with no reports to make. They wanted to speak to the inspector. They didn't say 'the inspector', actually, they asked for whoever was 'the boss'. They sat in the waiting room, locked in a silence that got heavier and heavier. For this reason, Officer Antonio Genovesi had already come into his room at least three times: there were a number of 'non-EU citizens', all with a folded piece of paper in their hand, who wanted to talk to him. More women than men. He added that no one looked like they had any intention of going anywhere, even though he'd tried to clear them out, 'nicely', he said, trying to gauge whether he should try a different, more energetic tack.

The only thing they could do was let them in. 'At least that way, we'll understand, right?' Inspector Vitale said at last, not wanting to deal with any more pointless dramas.

The chaos began as soon as Genovesi opened the door, saying, 'Please, one at a time,' as if he were talking to children and not a crowd of adults pushing him out of their way, all brandishing the pieces of paper that a few moments ago they had been holding in their hands like relics. Now they were fluttering around in a tangle of arms and hands above his head, like crazy birds, in an ominous clamour that the inspector, still sitting in his chair, couldn't understand in the slightest.

'Calm down, please,' he tried to say, as the stream overflowed and rushed towards his desk.

That was when he first started to understand that the squares of paper fluttering around weren't 'papers', but photos. And they were all face, head and shoulder, or full length shots of children.

That these were mothers, fathers, brothers and sisters, who had come for news of their children, the inspector only realised when he found himself almost underneath a screaming woman leaning over his desk in an attempt to show him a newspaper clipping reporting the news of a child recovered at sea and buried in the town cemetery. She kept repeating, 'Mine, alive! My child!' Meanwhile, she pulled from the pocket of a man's jacket two sizes too big for her a colour photograph of her child taken on the day of his second birthday in an Arabesque setting with colourful rugs and curtains, and then one of the identikits, whose image, albeit faded, was surprisingly similar, he couldn't dispute that.

The others, fathers, brothers and sisters, grandparents, mothers, were now saying the exact same thing: 'Mine, alive, mine!' despite the fact that their siblings, children and grandchildren had been recovered at sea, identified, buried, even taken to other cemeteries on the island. And they were all crying tears of joy as they spoke.

That was how things had gone on 28 October, the day that ended up shaking convictions and certainties on which Inspector Vitale had based his every thought and action: reality is reality; fantasies are fantasies. And he was a reality man – he was used to being pragmatic.

The next morning, the child perched on the television set had vanished without a trace.

While they didn't know exactly what had happened in their houses, miles away from each other, that night of 31 October 2020, none of the three, least of all Inspector Vitale, thought for one second that they had seen a ghost.

23

Textile district of Prato to Rome, 31 October

In the van, which left the motorway a while ago, turning towards the yellow lights of a junction leading straight to the city where Khaled knows he has to get out, it turns a lot colder than he expected.

A couple of years ago, he had passed through here, or hereabouts, on the journey to Europe. He didn't know where exactly this Europe began, where he and Nadir were heading. He'd imagined a long journey in the lorry they boarded not far from home, and, after a few days, Europe, where there was someone waiting to give them a job on a building site. That's what they'd told him. If his mother had even imagined the things they had to go through, the filthy places they ended up, the kicks and punches, the guns pushing them into the middle of the sea, the swollen eyes of his friend Hakan ... she would never have made them leave. He's sure of that. If not, she wouldn't be his mother.

He still finds it mind-boggling. For him 'Europe' is where Padre Buono is. End of story. The rest is ... whatever it is. Racking your brain doesn't do any good. That's why he's concentrating on the one thing he knows for sure: he has to keep going south, right to the end, to the point where the land finishes and the sea begins. 'My sea,' he tells himself, when he feels lost. Beyond that, somewhere, is his house, and there, waiting for him, his mother, Leila, his grandmother, Samira, and maybe even his father, Salim. 'God sends almonds to those with no teeth,' his grandmother used to say, proudly displaying her full set of teeth.

This thing where he thinks so intensely about what he misses almost makes him cry, even though he'd promised himself he would never cry.

And anyway, a couple of years ago when he passed through this area, it had been warm: the sun was as bright and hot as the day he'd set off with Nadir. In a basket, he had enough food for a few days and, sewn into the waistband of his trousers, a cloth bag with the money his mother had managed to borrow. 'I'll work and pay them back.' He was thinking about that the whole time he was in the tipper of the dumper truck that took them to the pick-up point where the journey would begin. He was crouched beside his brother, who kept staring back down the road clouded in black exhaust smoke. 'I'm not crying,' he said. And actually, he wasn't crying, even though it was a huge effort not to let a single tear fall from his eye, as the truck jolted and jerked between potholes, splashing up yellowish mud. Then Nadir came up close to his side and slid his head under his arm. He did the last stretch with his brother lying on top of him, unsure how exactly to hold a sleeping child.

Best not to think about it ... At least it's dark. That means Khaled can rub the back of his hand over his face without anyone noticing. This is all because of that pothole the truck went straight into, bringing back memories.

Khaled understands they've reached their destination from the way the Asian guy comes to a very decisive stop, pulling on the handbrake. A sharp manoeuvre, a violent whack to the back and neck.

Through the window, there are only dark silhouettes of buildings with their shutters closed tight and not a chink of light shining through. The place seems dead. Even the street lamps give off only a dim glow, and many of them don't even manage that. Where the glass cases are shattered but the bulbs are still intact, they look like burrs and luminous cobwebs. Only a scrawny dog is limping by near a wall.

When the guy opens the van window, Khaled can feel the cooler air, a cold that sends a shiver through him. Without a word, the man disappears, rummages in the back of the van, then comes back with a puffer coat and a hat that smell synthetic and new. He must have slipped them out of one of the packets they loaded in the city with the ghost factories. Khaled would like to say thank you or something along those lines, but he doesn't know the right language. So he bows his head, but the guy isn't there any more. He's standing at a door, waiting nervously. A shadowy figure emerges from a narrow gap. Inside, the light seems to be blinding white. It looks like a halo above the head of the thin man half visible through the swing doors.

This is where Khaled will spend the night. He understands this from the way the driver pushes him towards the entrance. Only when he walks through the door is the halo revealed for what it is: a sort of crown of grey hair that starts at the top of the old man's head and goes right down to his shoulders. It's hard to see how he can stand up; he seems like some kind of bird with long, incredibly thin legs as he walks towards a metal lift. When the doors close, it starts to go up slowly. So slowly that, at one point, Khaled wonders whether they will ever make it.

He can't bring the suitcase with him into the apartment, the old man explains. He has to leave it in a musty-smelling hallway with other stuff piled up against a wall, under some kind of coat rack stuffed with big jackets. He'll get it back when it's time to leave. And his shoes. He has to leave those there, too. At least that's the message he's getting. So Khaled pretends not to understand. He carries the suitcase in his arms. He doesn't let go even when the man tries to grab it, with what little strength he has.

If the guy from the van had been there too, things would probably have gone differently. Two of them could do it. They'd force him to leave his suitcase and shoes in the hallway. Maybe that's why the old man goes to the window. He opens it and looks down. Then, resigned, he snaps it shut. 'Come on then, you little fart,' he says in an Italian which conveys nothing to Khaled but his contempt.

The street below had been dark and dead, the exact opposite of the large room opening up before them, bathed in a dizzyingly bright white, or maybe it's the sudden roar that makes him woozy. A hiss like millions of trapped rattlesnakes. Trapped, like the people Khaled glimpses now and then between carts, spray guns, adjustable arms, presses: a few pairs of hands, a bit of a head, parts of shoulders, tufts of hair, calves, feet. A dozen pairs all told. All bare feet. Only one person by the entrance raises his head a little when he sees him come in, followed by the old man, who doesn't make eye contact with anybody. Everyone else is concentrating on their work. They move in the same way, with two or three robotic actions. Khaled focuses on one woman. He's still watching her take yet another rubber sole, spray it with glue and put it back on the cart chained to other carts that run one after the other on the track when the old man gestures for him to leave his stuff on the other side of a plasterboard wall.

If it hadn't been for the fact that the light came in there, barely screened, Khaled could easily have ended up walking into the camp beds lined up one beside the other. Ten, to be precise, where six men and four women are sleeping. Each curled up with their head under a pillow. Perhaps so they don't fall on the floor. Who knows. Even in there the noise is deafening, and the air is even more impossible to breathe: a mixture of glue, solvents, leather and digestion.

The guy from the van hasn't brought him here to sleep ... Khaled can tell that when the old man points out the sink in the corner, full of pots and pans, not far from some gas rings encrusted with food.

'Move it, flea,' he orders, with a snap of the head that Khaled is quick to understand. 'Hey, come on, move!'

If the old man had more strength in his legs, he would surely have given him a kick, instead it's just the nod. Padre Buono had been a thousand times better: when he had to hit someone, he hit them, and that was it. He didn't play the hard man, like this old guy here, who reeks of shit. Those guys are the most miserable miseries, according to his father. One time he'd told a bunch what he really thought of them, those leeches who acted big with machine guns and went around scaring people. 'God does not allow Himself to be enlisted!' His mother had never forgiven him. She said that was where the bad things started. She would tell herself that again and again, even after they ended up taking him away while she incredulously murmured the accusation levelled against her husband, Salim. 'A-pos-ta-sy ...'

When he rinses the last bowl under the icy water sputtering out of the tap, Khaled's hands are sore. They are so red that the skin between his fingers is cracked.

But the old man has antennae. As soon as Khaled finishes, he gets up from his seat and hands him a broom, to spare the workers' bare feet from remnants of plastic and leather, balls of twine, quantities of dust that never end but rather seem to get bigger, all congregating in his burning nostrils, making him sneeze, so starved of air that occasionally he feels like he's suffocating.

Khaled realises the worst thing of all after a while, when all he wants is to be able to collapse into a long sleep, anywhere, even under the workers' feet or on the conveyor belt, letting it move him around. It's that he will need to sweep and wash pots for many more hours yet, given that, after a certain amount of time that he can't calculate, the ten workers who were sleeping get up from the camp beds, without even needing to be told by the old man, who is napping in a chair with his chin resting on a walking stick. They come as they are, dragging themselves round the plasterboard to swap places with the others, who stretch their hands and legs then head to the bathroom (a toilet and sink) to wait their turn.

If Khaled had to say where this motley crew of workers came from, he wouldn't know where to start. The fact that no one speaks to anyone, and that the old man addresses everyone in the same obnoxious croaky voice and never gets an answer, the mechanical way they work, prepare food, curl up to sleep, drag themselves out of bed to go back to their places in front of the carts, reminds him of a film he'd seen when he was little. There were living people who were dead, or dead people who were alive, something like that. They had the same stiff walk.

Through the night, he kept jolting awake with a scream. As soon as he closed his eyes, he became one of them: who could tell if he was alive or dead? Even he didn't know. And that made him spring out of bed with his eyes wide open. Luckily, Nadir wasn't sleeping in the room with him, otherwise who knows how many days he would have spent asking him, 'Are you alive now, or are you still dead?'

24

Brussels, 31 October

In the end, Karolina dared. She went to the places she could never have imagined. Now she can stomach watching images that should horrify her, make her turn off the computer and unplug it forever. Yet she stays in this hell, looking for a clue, a face with a hint of her son's features. If that is where he ended up, as Fenna believes. Karolina hasn't heard from her since that night when she claimed to be 'sober as a newborn baby drinking milk' while she spewed the kind of bile Karolina would never have expected from her, against 'these Muslim extremist bastards' who were turning the country upside down, and the pricks who followed them, like Andreas.

She would never have expected such a venomous backlash from her friend. She didn't want an apology. But at least a sign, a 'How are you?' if nothing else, for the simple fact that she'd trusted her, confided in her about things she would never have dared share with anybody else.

'Because who else could you have told that your son had got screwed over by the *allah akbar* ... Well?' Now, Karolina can well imagine those words crossing Fenna's lips.

*

She prefers not to even think about it. She's better off keeping to herself and looking for Andreas on her own, even if that means ending up in the hell of propaganda videos.

She stops the images to look at the details of the eyes in the shot of a window of a truck screeching through the dust of a city in ruins. Iraq, Syria . . . She doesn't even know exactly where this is on the map. Tied to the bumper, lifeless puppets are dragged along like tin cans on a wedding car. She returns time and again to the close-up of fighters who, one after the other, pull knives from a block of wood: were it not for the colour of their beards and sometimes their irises, they could all be the same person in one photograph shown ad infinitum. It is this difficulty with identifying facial features that drives her crazy, making her rewatch the same videos, obsessed by any tiny detail that could give her confirmation of what she's looking for.

Sometimes, when she comes round, she starts to think she's not even doing it for Andreas any more, but that there's just some inexplicable, crazy force driving her to watch. Or, what's worse, that she likes it – it's horrifying, but she likes it. She also feels pure hatred. For everyone. In those moments, collapsed on the sofa, she even finds herself suspicious. The very idea of having reached this point drives her to despair. More than shame, she feels a frightening sense of loneliness: abandoned to her fate by everyone, even by herself.

The alternative would be to do nothing. To go to work, come home, let the hours go by, take her sleeping pills, get into bed and do it all again the next day. Until it drove her mad.

At one point this afternoon, however, something happens that she can't explain. She doesn't know how she ended up there. She isn't sure whether it's a social media page or a website. She follows the instructions. She chooses a username and password.

'Welcome' is the message that pops up in the chat window.

'My name is Karolina,' she types.

The response is instant: 'Welcome.' Maybe it's an automatic message, but it's quickly followed by a question: 'What brings you here?'

'I'm looking for my son,' she writes, without thinking. 'Andreas,' she adds and types his surname. 'He disappeared. I don't know where he's gone. Can you help me?' she continues mechanically, waiting for an answer that doesn't come.

This is why, after sitting for who knows how long staring at the cursor flashing away on the screen, unsure whether she should keep this thread of contact open or close everything down, she decides to stand up from her son's desk and leave the house.

She hadn't realised it had got dark outside. There aren't many people around on the wide roads with carefully sculpted hedges. The first Christmas lights, that someone has hung way in advance among the leaves and branches, help to mark out the green shape, since there are no street lamps nearby.

There are plenty of lights on inside houses that all look beautiful from the street. Fragments of ordinary lives through the large windows, where Karolina can see a woman busy preparing dinner, a girl's head resting on the sofa, a couple hugging. She can't tell whether it's a goodbye or a reunion at the end of the day. She can't even muster any nostalgia; that kind of affection has faded so far into her memory, over-whelmed by bad feelings: the all-too-vivid recollection of the yelling between father and son; punches against the door; and, in the end, the violently specific outbursts directed at her, for being 'the cause' of it all – this 'nothing' of a son she'd raised, 'good for nothing but eating and shitting', and 'that dick of a father' she'd married. All of it her fault, even the bruises she earned some nights, when she got caught in the middle trying to split them up.

She does feel longing. Longing to be inside one of those houses, cooking, waiting for someone to come home, or just to tidy up the things a son had left lying around so that she can drink tea in peace with a friend, nattering about this and that. That was it: she would like to be able to give herself that little break from life, feel the steam rush from a cup and warm her face. That's all.

A car glides down the road and stops in front of a garage door that slowly starts to open. Even that shutter movement, the purr of the waiting engine and then the caution with which the car drives inside seems desirable. It's too bad she doesn't have a car, never mind a garage, otherwise she'd go for a drive on her own just to be able to come home and press the button on the remote control to give herself that 'welcome home' moment.

The moon is too clouded over for its sometimes silvery glow to compete with the yellow of the street lamps. Looking at it carefully, it seems like the face of a witch appearing from behind tattered clouds to ruin the nice thoughts she'd managed to summon up.

There's one bar open on the corner of the little square from where the buses leave for the city centre during the day.

At this hour, she wouldn't have expected to find so many people in a place that, from the outside, looks like the waiting room of an out-of-the-way train station from another time. Even the huge wooden tables, with long, deep cracks running through them, look like they've been dredged up from some remote place no one can remember the first thing about. Karolina surprisingly likes it there, despite being more comfortable in places that feel like they have – or are in – space, places like Liège Station, a spaceship that seems to have landed on Earth direct from Mars. That too, in its own way, is from another time.

The crackle of the television, hanging from the ceiling on a cable, plunges her back into the one dimension she doesn't want to be in: the present, with its bad news and anxious days.

Fortunately, it's not the news that people are glued to but a football match.

Taking a seat next to a man and a woman, both alone and drinking a pilsner, she turns her attention to the tiny figures running across the bright green field as she waits for her beer.

She can't tell how much anyone's really interested in the football and how much they're just looking for a place where they can surround themselves with people. A woman who must be Karolina's age is getting involved, celebrating and despairing with a passion that seems unnatural, coming out with occasional comments that no one acknowledges, except the waitress who smiles and nods when she brings over another bottle.

There is also an unnatural sadness to the way she says, 'It's over,' when the referee blows his whistle, and the unease she can't quite hide as she drinks the last drop and rifles through her handbag for her purse, while everyone around her stands up and someone changes the channel.

Karolina is also waiting for the waitress to bring her bill. She hopes that no one watching sees her the way she sees that woman: lost and helpless. Actually, she hopes nobody notices her at all, or the worm that has burrowed into her brain, ready to regurgitate all her thoughts.

On the screen now, there's a fat guy trying to answer a question a journalist had asked him a moment ago.

It only becomes clear what they're talking about when the interviewer recaps his story. It seems to be something to do with a thing the guy saw in the middle of the fog at the back of a lay-by not far from the motorway, where he stopped his lorry a couple of months ago to stretch his legs.

'A red creature, floating,' the driver explained. 'And then it disappeared.'

When the journalist asks if he believes in ghosts, the man shrugs. He doesn't know what to say.

The next person interviewed is also a lorry driver. His reconstruction is very precise and leaves no room for doubt: the boy he gave a lift to had a suitcase with him, but he doesn't say what colour it was. He can't remember.

'Very heavy,' he says ominously, nervously touching his reddening bald head.

'Probably,' he adds, sounding decisive, as soon as the interviewer asks the question everyone is waiting for. 'Guns, knives, stuff like that. Probably, yes.' He shows the trolley the offender was pulling, which he'd left in the lorry's cabin. What he definitely can say is that the bastard must have been thirteen, fourteen years old, fifteen at most. When he'd got out to go for a pee, he'd tried to steal his wallet from his pocket.

'Any other details?'

'None, except the fact that the immigrant bastard is going around with a dagger or a flick knife . . . a blade like this.' He holds his hands apart to demonstrate. It's a miracle his throat hadn't been slit.

Since the sad woman closed her bag and got up to go back to her own life, Karolina has been consumed by a single thought: going home to check the chat window. This is how she misses the sarcastic joke with which the TV presenter wraps up the final local news bulletin.

'Now, given that the events happened on more or less the same day and in areas not that far apart, the question we have to ask, and I think legitimately, is how a floating creature, a little red ghost, would be able to rob a fully grown lorry driver at knife point.'

The rest Karolina half listened to, without paying any attention to the details which, had she caught them, would have only added to her worries.

25

Po valley, Emilia-Romagna, 2 November

Tension was running through the whole country now, like an electric current underground. It's not that people were, on the whole, inclined to give any serious consideration to this story about 'live children' and the parents desperately looking for them, which was circulating mainly on the internet. Many were actually making jokes about the mental wellbeing of people who were still being 'led by the nose'. Someone even asked whether the elusive Sicilian office of the major national newspaper that broke the story was in fact non-existent, which none of the editors bothered to confirm or deny. A couple of morning and afternoon talk shows had already picked up on the topic. During one of these programmes, the question at the bottom of the screen read: OUTSIDERS. REALITY OR PSYCHOSIS?

'That stuff's for housewives, old folk and southern tabloids,' commented one guest, who showed 'no respect for people and a whole part of the country', the host was quick to remark, with an apology to her devoted audience for the offence and 'thoughtlessness', she felt the need to point out.

In some regions in the south and in the north, what became apparent was the strengthening of powers for the police and neighbourhood services, set out in plans for coordinated control of national territory. It was revealed that a confidential report was doing the rounds in certain commands. What exactly it was about, however, remained a mystery.

The incident that generated the most confusion on social media actually took place in the autumn when schools opened, and it was dredged up by a television show that prided itself on its serious approach, although its ratings had been falling for a while. The incident could be described in a few lines: on their first day back, children at a primary school were met by a bank of green desks with dozens of rats writhing around on top. The hysterical screams mixed with desperate squeaks echoed from classroom to classroom. It was a horror or an omen that had made more than one viewer call for immediate vaccinations for the entire school population against leptospirosis, seeing as the caretaker's dog had caught it. Liver and kidneys fucked. Fever, vomiting, dehydration, jaundice ... The caretaker never had the courage to admit that it was a stunt pulled by his son (glue traps on the desks) to get revenge for the death of his dog, which had actually happened a few days earlier. This strengthened the idea in many people's minds that for some time the peninsula had been overrun by creatures capable of slipping into schools without breaking doors or windows.

That the concern had crossed borders, with the local police being alerted, was not yet public knowledge, but in some cities, especially in the Brussels area, measures had been taken to tighten security in primary and secondary schools, and empty whole areas and municipalities that had until that point been considered 'probable jihadist hotspots'.

'Antiterrorist measures as part of prevention activities' was the official line on the decision to start a census of unaccompanied minors in reception centres. This conveniently ignored a universally uncomfortable truth: those centres only housed the kids who hadn't managed to sneak under the radar by immersing themselves deep in the underworld. The occasional news that did emerge about the others involved exploitation and unspeakable trades – but then again, the reception centres were no guarantee against the destiny of falling into a life of crime.

Some countries further strengthened the presence at their effectively restored borders. At certain points, military blockades were set up, since this business seemed to have something to do with the waves of refugees and migrants sweeping through the south and east of Europe.

One person who believed that the story about 'illegals' – as told by the former teacher with a history of neighbourhood-watch patrols – should be given serious consideration, and who therefore brought it to the table of the national executive, was the regional secretary of the party that put the safety of citizens first – citizens, he was quick to point out, of 'Veneto, Lombardy and Padua'. To be absolutely clear.

The terms in which he presented the matter to the national secretary – linking it to the mysterious bruises on the arms of children in San Zenone and the leptospirosis that could have infected entire school populations in the Po valley – were not much different to those used by the journalist who, from the television programme dedicated to the former teacher hunting down children who 'slipped through' his fingers 'li-te-ra-lly', had gained a certain notoriety.

'*They might not even exist* ... but *people's fear does exist*. And we take that seriously.'

Those words struck a chord with the party leader, who quickly drew the necessary conclusions, employing the politically beneficial phrase 'two birds with one stone'. Who gave a shit if they were real or plausible or fake! The events in question were confirmation of what he'd been saying for years: this migrant invasion was jeopardising people's lives, paving the way – and this was the interesting part – for the uncharted territory of consensus within the party. These were the two birds. The stone was an initial decision that, although it didn't refer explicitly to any of these stories, did give a clear signal. 'A free hand for the police and carabinieri,' he announced, promising sweet dreams for all children, although he had no children himself, nor intended to bring any into the world, as he jokingly told supporters.

The priest in the national secretary's home parish, in Treviso, who in no way agreed with his former altar boy's way of doing things, and, moreover, had taken to heart the fate of one Senegalese couple ('Good people, Luchin, it makes no sense that they shouldn't exist on this Earth . . .'), eventually received the most genuine answer someone like that can give: 'Who says, Don Egidio, that they should not exist? I say we need them to exist, they absolutely have to exist . . .' His words had an unintentionally sinister tone.

Orso didn't believe in the ghosts from these rumours that had been buzzing around the Po valley for a while, or in any of that sort of rubbish, but he did believe in order, surveillance and vigilance. So he was pleased when he heard about the stance taken by the regional secretary and then the leader of his preferred party.

As a retired security guard, he trusted in only a few, very tangible, things : the green beret he'd been wearing since he was a boy, the khaki Punto that had never let him down, and his old faithful Beretta 98FS. He also kept a hunting rifle under his bed, a 12-gauge Beretta 151 with the pipe cleaner kit for cleaning the barrel and raw linseed oil for polishing the stock.

Since his wife died, he liked to think he might meet her every now and then in his dreams, even though he hadn't been able to remember his dreams for a long while. He never shared this fantasy with anyone. He'd been careful not to, even on the couple of nights a week he spent at the bar, when, what with all the talking, and the blood rushing to his head as soon as they got on to the state of the country, he'd end up tipsy. Never drunk.

He'd thrown out the last television a couple of years ago. It was broken and he hadn't wanted to buy another just so he could listen to bullshit from morning to night. 'You always find out the news, one way or another,' he would tell anyone who made fun of him, always repeating the same joke: 'Orso: bear by name, bear by nature.'

At the bar that night, they'd really harped on about the story of these wandering minors. The owner, who served all the drinks himself, had even shown them a couple of YouTube videos. Teachers and parents were asking for better surveillance, day and night, around schools and on the streets in the Po valley. Lads with sculpted hair had volunteered their services. Someone had even made a digital representation of the red creature that a Belgian lorry driver had reported floating in the mist. That had happened in the Po valley, too, according to the caption.

Orso made his way home, disgruntled. What a crap night! A couple of times he even found himself reaching for the glovebox where he kept the Berretta, trying to stop his heart racing. On a particularly dark bend, the beam of the headlights suddenly lit up a broken branch, hanging down crooked into the road. Instinctively, Orso leaned towards the glove compartment to grab his pistol, when it would have been better just to swerve out of the way. On a straight stretch of road, which had recently been resurfaced, he was so focused on the hypnotic white line in the middle of the pitch-black tarmac and the darkness of the night that, at one point, he got the impression that someone had swiped the road, leaving just this bright white streak in the middle of nothing.

Now that he was arriving home, he also had to wrestle with the lock that had, without fail, been ruining his day and his mood for over a month.

His 'expat' neighbour, who, after a lifetime working his arse off in America, had decided to move back to live within 500 metres of his house, had that night – the dickhead – started up with the Christmas decorations, over a month ahead of what was, for Orso, the lousiest time of the year: usually from 8 December until 7 January, when the bastard finally took the decorations down and stopped 'intermittently' pissing him off.

He barely has time to brake on the dirt track beyond the gate and scramble out of the Punto, so furious that he almost falls over.

At his feet, Lupo keeps barking like a thing possessed. He's running to and fro between the storage shed and his master's boots, not giving a damn about being called to heel, when he's usually such a good soldier and follows orders without a peep.

Orso is quick to go inside, take the rifle from under his bed and load it, fearing that the Beretta might not be enough.

How a fox or some other animal has got into the shed, he has no idea, seeing as he's sure he left the door and the only window locked. Yes – he had. Even the padlock is in place. There's been no attempt to break and enter, but still Lupo is going crazy, scratching at the wooden door, trying to dig a hole to open up a gap, whining.

This is no mouse, Orso can tell. Lupo doesn't give a shit about mice.

So the decision is made. He turns the key in the padlock, which sticks because of the frost, and opens.

Before he can even switch on the light, Lupo dives inside, with a clatter of tools, tins, piles of stuff tumbling everywhere.

Orso quickly leans forward, the way he ducks into the bushes when they're out hunting. He can't turn round and switch on the light in case there's really something, or someone, hiding in there that could jump him from behind.

'Show yourself!' he growls through his perfectly aligned false teeth that make him feel as strong as he did in his youth. 'Come out, shitface! So Orso can get you. And if Orso doesn't get you, Lupo will drag you outside. Right, Lupo?' he calls to the dog, who is now barking loudly.

26

Rome, 2 November

Khaled would have beaten him to death with that stick, if one of the younger workers hadn't stopped him, grabbing him by the waist and lifting him off the ground.

The old shitbag must have realised he was ready to let fly another blow to his already bleeding head. That's why he lifted his wrinkly arm up to the stick that he'd been dozing on just seconds earlier. Khaled didn't understand what he said. His voice came out in a squawk.

All the workers, even the ones who'd been sleeping, have rushed to the entrance. Until that moment, the night had been like every other night, presided over by the body of their old friend snoozing in his chair. Now there's no one working at the conveyor belt, where the carts keep circling, empty, in the incessant din. The work that goes on there, day and night, has been reduced to nothing but the machinery and sleep-denying light that seems even more dense and angry.

If the mechanical roar should stop for a moment, the room would be in stony silence, now that the old man is a frightened bag of bones on the floor, and Khaled has finally put down the stick. One of the younger workers decides to do what none of the others would even have dared think about. Crouched in front of the old man's body, he rifles through his trouser pockets, looking for the key that, after a moment, slides onto the floor from some hidden fold.

Khaled pounces and grabs it. When he unlocks the door to the entrance where the jackets are hanging above orderly lines of shoes, no one follows him, except the young worker, who motions frantically, as if to say, 'Hurry up!'

Everyone else is staring in silence. Behind them the machinery goes blindly on; at their feet, the old man twists his neck in an extreme effort to stop these two with the power of his stare. Hard and intense, but still the look of someone who knows he will pay dearly.

The thought of the suitcase strikes Khaled like the lash of a whip a second before he closes the door behind him. So he turns back, with the young worker yelling after him.

He strides confidently, but doesn't run, towards the dormitory. When he emerges from behind the board, life in the room has resumed its normal rhythm. The workers have gone back to their carts, concentrating on the shoes running along the belt at the usual, regular speed. They don't turn to watch him walk towards the exit, where two middle-aged workers are leaning over the old man. They both speak their own language, each to herself, as they help the man back to his feet.

The last thing Khaled notices, before he leaves, is the way the two women treat the old man, with a sort of timid apprehension: as though their very existence depended on that beaten, skinny body, and on the stick, which the old man points to, because they pick it up instantly and hand it to him.

It's one, maybe two in the morning. Someone must have smashed more of the lamps up the street, because to Khaled the neighbourhood seems even more embalmed in darkness than it was two days ago. Maybe even longer has passed. He couldn't say. The cold is bitter. Even though Khaled's wearing the jacket from the discount store as well as the electric-blue puffer coat that Asian bastard had given him before he handed him over to the old man, and even though he's running frantically behind the worker, who seems to know exactly where to go, he still can't warm up properly. He feels a fever come over his muscles and bones. It's a sensation he's only experienced once before in his life: the time he'd seen his friend Hakan beaten to death, the day before they got on board an enormous white tyre that already seemed to be sinking in the shallow water, as Nadir reached for his hand. 'Let's go home,' he'd pleaded in a whisper, trying not to be heard by the gun barrels pointing at their backs to keep them moving *Forward!*

'Stop!' The boy suddenly grabs hold of his arm. 'Stop!' he repeats, looking up at a building on the corner. It's not because of the flashing yellow traffic light. He's showing Khaled a camera pointing at the street. 'Put your hood up,' he orders, pulling on his wool hat. 'Put it up! Those things can see right into your pants!' he says, pointing out the flashing red light again. Then Khaled understands. But he doesn't follow the boy's order. He takes off his coat.

'What the fuck are you doing?'

He takes off his jacket too. He covers the suitcase and carries it in his arms.

'Are you completely nuts? I told you to put that hood on your head!' He whips the blue coat off the suitcase, forces him to put it back on.

Carrying the suitcase covered by the jacket, and with the blue hood pulled down until it almost covers his eyes, Khaled keeps following the boy, who's crossing the road with his hands in his pockets as if the eyes of the world are on him, even though there isn't another living soul in sight. Meanwhile, he's struggling along with the suitcase in his arms, weaving all over the place. He almost collapses when they finally get on the bus.

'Will you put that down!'

Khaled shakes his head in a 'no' that leaves no room for argument. Even sitting down, he clutches it tightly to his belly.

Now the cold accumulated in his body starts to thaw, the humid warmth mixed with sweat sticks his clothes to his skin. He's exhausted and he needs to sleep. Even the boy sitting in front of him seems worn out. He's resting his head on the window, where a halo has formed, growing smaller and bigger with the rhythm of his breathing. He's not as hard-nosed now as he had been when he told the others, 'You lot can die here. I'm getting out. Send my regards to the shoemaker,' in an Italian that sounded similar to the way the old man spoke, but less fluent.

Khaled, slumped in his seat with his eyelids drooping, insists on watching him. He's sure that if he wasn't there to stare at him, the boy would burst into tears. He can tell from the way he's pressing his forehead into the glass and how he screws up his face, sniffing.

'You can't do this to me now,' Khaled thinks, without taking his eyes off him, even though he can barely keep them open after so few hours of poor-quality sleep stolen between one shift and the next.

'I'm watching you. I'm watching you,' he keeps repeating to himself, as if the power of his thoughts were strong enough for himself and the other kid, who's still pressing his head against the window, but he doesn't crack. In fact, after half an hour, he jumps to his feet.

'Oi, we have to get off,' he says, making his way to the doors as they open onto a flat building flooded with light that to Khaled seems monstrously huge. Like something from another planet.

The expanse of light dominated by a giant sign is not where they're going, though.

'Follow me, come on,' the boy says, ducking into a side street, pulling Khaled by the hand, while he pulls the suitcase with the other. It looks like a tortoise under the jacket, or an elephant-dog, because of the sleeves that dangle down and get stuck in the wheels.

'We're here!'

The boy is now pointing to a grate that looks like the entrance to a sewer.

'You'll be okay here.'

He lifts it up and slips inside.

Khaled couldn't have imagined that he'd see so many eyes down there in a sea of legs, arms, heads and scraps of blankets. All of them, together, staring at him.

'Where's my friend?' the boy asks.

Nothing stirs among the brown mass of bodies and blankets. Out of the dark tunnel comes a solitary voice: 'There's no room here!' But it quickly falls silent.

Khaled can make out some slow, blind movement. It reminds him of the worms his dad used to keep in a tin when they went fishing. Then he spies a shape twisting around, making a path through this bait box, emerging bit by bit until it takes the form of a skinny figure squinting, dumbstruck, from under protruding brow bones.

'Where did you end up?' he exclaims. Without waiting for an answer, he greets the boy with a fierce hug. 'I thought you were a goner.'

'Right,' says the boy, twisting his face into a look that's meant to be ironic. 'I'm back from the dead. I just came to see you because I'm leaving.'

'Oh, don't listen to him. There's room. For you,' the new kid clarifies.

'Then give my place to my friend here. He's here for a while. For a while,' he repeats, making his request sound very specific, as if he's saying, 'Don't let anything happen to him.'

The kid nods. 'Trust me.'

Now it's the boy's turn to throw his arms around him, in a clinch that seems almost desperate. 'Don't let yourself get screwed over for the shoemaker's money. Steer clear of him. Don't get screwed over.' Then he turns to Khaled and gives him a pat on the back. 'Thanks, yeah,' he says. 'I was going mad as a box of frogs in there . . . Okay.'

He sets off out of the tunnel, but turns around. 'It's getting ugly out there,' he says, pointing in the general direction of the city above.

His friend shrugs. 'We don't know anything about that here.'

'Just be careful.'

Only at the last moment does he raise his hand to wave, but he doesn't look back.

27

Brussels, 2 November – 8 December

She's been typing the same string of words for ages now, without getting any response.

'My name is Karolina. I'm looking for my son. Andreas. He disappeared. I don't know where he's gone. Can you help me?'

She's so far from the world, and herself, that she has no idea how much the news stories reported a couple of days ago have moved on: the red creature floating in the mist near the motorway, and the boy who asked for a lift with the lorry driver, just to *slit his throat and take possession of the vehicle*, as the victim of the attack was now claiming – highlighting the detail that made the migrant's actions all the more despicable, which was that the unsuspecting lorry driver only got out of the truck to relieve himself after hours of driving.

Despite the conflicts of jurisdiction between the police's nineteen different municipalities in Brussels-Capital and the six interzones, the differences between Walloon and Flemish territories, contradictions between legal provisions to be issued in Dutch or in French, conflict that threatened to hold up every measure ... orders from the very top of the security services had mobilised officers from federal and local police forces to conduct an in-depth investigation into the possible links between the two stories.

What had put the superintendent of the Brussels West Department – one of the six interzones of the Brussels police – on the alert, after his awful night in front of the television with that kid staring at him, unfazed, was the detail about the unidentified red creature. He wanted quick and detailed investigations, especially considering the 'wandering minors' arriving from the other end of the continent, meaning from southern Europe, which for him was the source of all evil and nightmares: so many drownings that he had lost track of the number, or scale; mass landings, which had multiplied beyond measure since a cork had been plugged in the Balkan route; nonchalance and failings by the forces that presided over those territories with a wide – very wide – mesh net, as everyone knew; and borders that, in that part of Europe, were like sieves for illegal migrants, terrorists and corrupt guards and customs officials. He was still racking his brain trying to remember the colour of the T-shirt hanging untidily off the boy. He couldn't say for sure that it wasn't red, albeit very faded.

None of this has managed to penetrate the secure boundaries of the world on which Karolina is pinning her remaining hopes.

'My name is Karolina. I'm looking for my son. Andreas. He disappeared. I don't know where he's gone. Can you help me?'

Sometimes she writes the words with enthusiasm, as if she is typing them for the first time. Other times carefully, slowly, almost seeking comfort in those words alone, without nurturing any hopes, determined never to do it again.

*

The question pops up in her chat window when her thoughts have turned to how stupid she's been to write such personal details on a site that, really, she knew nothing about.

'Who are you?'

It takes a moment for Karolina to realise that, at last, the thing she never dared imagine has happened.

'His mother,' she types shakily.

'Andreas's mother?'

The very fact that whoever is writing these messages remembers her son's name brings a joy she can't even conceive, let alone recall the last time she felt it.

'Yes,' she types, without adding anything more. Then, impatient, she puts three dots to fill the silence of the answer that doesn't come.

'Good,' appears in the box on the screen.

'Good. Yes.' She'd initially added an exclamation mark to that line, but deleted it before she hit send, so as not to betray her feelings.

She waits a few minutes for a sign from the other party to tear her away from the cursor flashing next to the monosyllabic 'yes', which seems to have ended the conversation.

'I love him so much,' she starts typing. Then, afraid of the silence again, she goes on. 'I miss him. I'd like to hold his hands. He knows. We used to do that. Will you pass that on, please, to my son?' Her fingers on the keyboard express emotion that, at one point, swells into a wave of anger and shame, because of the silence that follows her every word. She would like to write: *Who are you? Why don't you let me talk to my son? Why should I keep telling you these things? I need to speak to him. Where is he? Why won't he come back? Tell him!* Instead, the fear of losing this thread of hope too dictates a line that takes a lot for her to write, as she types it, with that final dizziness: 'Lots of love. Wherever you are.'

The conversation seems to be over. But just as she decides to move away, a sequence of words appears on the screen that Karolina keeps on rereading, even when she's convinced that nothing else will happen, not this afternoon.

'I love you so much, my only mum. *Your son, Andreas.*' This last part is written like a signature.

She knows her son could never put together a sentence like that. Not even if he was trying to be sarcastic. She ought to feel like someone has tricked her or, more simply put, taken the piss out of her, but instead she lets those words roll around her empty brain.

For the first time in months, that night she goes into the kitchen to prepare a proper dinner. She defrosts the rabbit she bought in February when she still thought Andreas would come home in a few days. She lays out all the ingredients she needs on the table: butter, prunes, beer, onions, thyme, cloves, bay leaves and a piece of bread covered in strong mustard.

It's not that this is Andreas's favourite meal. It was just one of the things he liked to eat, that's all. But she loves it, and she loves making it the way her grandmother taught her. She loves slow cooking on a low heat, waiting for the meat to soften and the beer to turn into a sweet sauce.

'Too fatty, that stuff,' her ex-husband used to say. 'Too fatty, that stuff.' And perhaps that was his way of saying that she was too fat, on top of everything else. But tonight, even that thought, which should make her feel like the saddest, most undesirable woman, unexpectedly makes her happy. 'Too fatty, that stuff. Too fatty,' she repeats in a voice like an out-of-tune trombone, as she browns the meat in the butter, filling the kitchen with a welcoming smell, a kind of warmth that, once it gets into the nose, gradually spreads to the whole body.

After dinner, which keeps her company until late, there is the promise – like every night – of sleep. A synthetic, drug-induced sleep, but at least it will last until morning.

For the first time since she started working at the estate agency, she hadn't woken up on time. There was nothing she could do. She was going to be a good half an hour late, but knowing that didn't throw her into a panic. It meant she would clean everything, just not as well as usual. 'That way, they'll have less to mess up,' she said, laughing as she automatically made her way to her son's room.

Only when she opens the door and looks into Andreas's world, just the way he left it months ago, does she feel bewildered for a moment. Standing in the doorway, she closes her eyes. When she opens them again, she is outside the room.

For today, she hopes she can manage not to think about it, and hold on to that 'I love you so much, my only mum', so far-fetched and babyish that, another time, it would have left her deeply ashamed. Even shaking off her embarrassment like this makes her feel good, insofar as anything can make her feel good.

A month later, when she receives a phone call from the discount store about a loyalty card or something, the euphoria has been absent for days.

She has gone back to living glued to those brief, perfunctory, disembodied messages, with no real conviction that this virtual contact is actually bringing her any closer to her son.

She still goes to the discount store to buy the few bits she needs, and also because, in this life, you never know. Not that she's harbouring any hopes of seeing that boy again, the last person who had made her feel like she could do something for someone. But still she goes, and every time she walks down the biscuit, cereal and waffle aisle. She doesn't buy cookies any more.

It gives her a sad and hopeless feeling to see them drying out on the scalloped-edge saucer beside the computer.

The phone call takes her by surprise on her way home from work. Just the fact that anyone's calling her on her mobile – which she now leaves in her bag like a forgotten object, even though she charges it every evening, like clockwork, in case her son tries to contact her during the night – seems like a good sign.

She immediately thinks of Fenna, and that an apology would be overdue but welcome, so welcome.

The screen shows 'number withheld'. She answers anyway, even though she can already envisage herself arguing with some call centre. And she answers in a tone that would encourage anyone to start chatting, even with a stranger.

On the other end of the line is a polite young woman. Karolina likes the jovial way she asks, 'Did you happen to keep the receipt from the shopping you did on ...?' She gives her a specific date that Karolina remembers perfectly. She's not someone who keeps receipts, but she still has that one in her wallet, for luck.

'I think so,' she says. 'Why?' The question comes out with a weight of expectation, even though that makes no sense.

'Because ...' The woman stops for a second. 'Well, for two reasons: one, in case you wanted to exchange it, exchange the suitcase, I mean, or if there were any problems with the buckle ... a few customers have had that happen.'

'I don't need to exchange it.'

'But if you did ...'

'I don't,' Karolina insists, indignant at what feels like someone trying to snatch a happy little memory away from her. 'It's fine where it is.'

'Of course,' the woman says, keeping her tone polite. 'But,' she adds, quickly changing tack, 'do keep it, that receipt, because we're raffling off a prize, a lottery we call it, for people who did their shopping that day.'

Karolina says nothing.

The woman senses her mood and tries to press on. 'We picked a date out of a hat for the month of September, and that's the date that came out,' she tries to explain, her nerves seeming to get the better of her slightly. 'I just wanted to let you know. We're doing the same with all our cardholders,' she adds. 'Anyway, you have a good afternoon,' she says as if she has no more time, or inclination, to talk.

Karolina returns the platitude. She's not sure if the woman is still on the line, though.

28

Po valley, Emilia-Romagna,
6 November – 8 December

Since the night he left, saying, 'I wouldn't believe this bullshit about ghosts even if I saw one in the flesh sat in my armchair in front of the fire,' Orso hadn't been seen at the bar.

Everyone had something to say about it. The argument had started as a game, just something to pass the time. Some people thought it was the owner's fault for making fun of him. 'If these ghosts have flesh, we can make a nice soup out of them!' he'd said, mocking the nonsense Orso was coming out with. Others thought it was quite normal – the old man had caught a whiff of festive spirit and hunkered down at home like he did every year. 'So he's starting a month early?' asked the bar owner, who never missed a chance to have a dig at 'that Orso', who he didn't like at all. 'Stubborn as a mule. There's no talking to him ...' Others thought Orso had been taken ill, a touch of bronchitis or the like, given that the last time he'd gone to what they all called the 'pre-war grocer's' he'd bought milk and honey. And his voice had been hoarse and frightening. But one guy said he must be fine, because no more than three days ago, he'd made it as far as the hardware store. He'd wanted poison and glue for mice. 'His hobby!' he mocked, referring to Orso's obsession with the mice that unfailingly managed to flatten themselves enough to get into his shed and drive him mad.

Some people wrote him off as a 'senile old boozehound', getting a rise out of the older drinkers, who weren't in the business of dismissing people like that, just because they'd had their troubles and had to contend with old age and loneliness. 'In his youth, that man could kill a bull with his bare hands,' they chorused, rapping their knuckles on their heads. 'And still could, if he wanted ... Never mind soup ... He'll eat them alive, all those gyppos ... Because that's what this is about, nothing to do with ghosts! These politicians with their fancy policies, bunch of pricks!' they exclaimed, casting glances at the group of lads playing on the machines: the ones who were most fired up by this story of so-called 'presences', or 'entities'.

It was one of them who'd told them that, a few years ago, he'd seen one with his own eyes. Not a little child, but a pregnant woman, dressed in a white skirt, with bare feet. She was standing in the middle of a car park, staring into space. At four in the morning. On the kind of night that tempted out werewolves. He'd seen her standing like a sculpture in the headlight of his motorbike. 'That is a fucked-up memory.'

'So these must be that bitch's children,' the youngest had scoffed, only half joking.

Another claimed that something similar had happened to his ex on holiday. Night had fallen and she and her friends turned on the light on their phones because at one point there were really weird noises and calls all around, like animals, and babies crying. 'Triple scary!' he admitted.

The one who was kind of the leader of the group, Rambo 2 (because Rambo 1 was Stallone, end of story), had a more scientific explanation for why these 'presences' existed ... He wasn't open to debate. He'd found a firm online that sold a video camera that protected against any kind of intruder, perceptible or imperceptible, 'Which would even include presences,' he explained. That had to mean something!

It had been a few weeks since anyone mentioned Orso. Attention had been focused on an article in the journal published by the party that had the safety of citizens in the Po valley at heart.

It praised the prophetic spirit of communities that had been able to predict what had, for some time, been keeping people awake at night – decent people, it discreetly but very eloquently stressed. Whoever or whatever was causing this commotion could not possibly be decent. This was the meaning that all loyal readers inferred without it needing to be spelled out.

The public mood was behind the newspaper and the party, which, since the story of the 'illegals' began, had seen their popularity grow, as predicted by the national secretary and his nose for these things.

The 'prophetic spirit' referred to the strength with which the community, in simpler times, had made an unsentimental objection to the presence of families of 'undocumented migrants' in their territory, which, in current terminology, they called 'their house'.

Their 'house' was the church, where the priest had timidly tried to put up a resistance to the protests by offering to provide a roof for a few months to four women with a couple of babies in tow. He'd been 'forced by who knows what powers'. Some churchgoers said that they wouldn't let the old parish priest be treated like that, preferring instead to use some good old-fashioned blackmail of their own.

Their 'house' was also the police station, where someone had suggested, given the emergency, that they should put up a couple of families in tents in the forecourt, after a terrifying shipwreck that had littered the country's southern coastline with bodies. News to which the party journal had dedicated a paragraph. *Innocent victims of traffickers and do-gooders* was the headline that caused controversy up and down the country, controversy that didn't actually dissuade the 'local communities' from fighting against this invasion of people who were too different and too out of place in this part of the Po valley, which already had its own problems and innocent victims – its own people in need.

According to the latest news, no one in this municipality had complained about the presence of 'undocumented ghosts', the columnist points out with a hint of irony. He is a well-known writer, famed for the consistency with which he has always defended the interests of his fellow citizens claiming no more nor less than 'the natural right to be masters of their own homes, and to save the white, Christian race from extinction'.

So no one could deny the 'clear' connection between the two things: migrants with families in tow, and minors roaming around. Besides, the more forward-looking among them had even said, and written in their comments on the online edition of the journal, that these groups of 'extended families' and 'apparently defenceless women' were only the 'first wave' in a tide that would soon have quite different proportions if they carried on like this, telling everyone to 'come on in and make yourselves at home'.

The article, which the owner of the bar had pinned to the wall, had sparked days of increasingly vocal debate, with the boys in the bar maintaining that this was a way to distract attention from the number-one issue. And the number-one issue, which plenty of people had addressed, but no one had ever got to the bottom of, was the presence of that gypsy camp not far from the motorway, which was where the 'rats' came from, the 'lice' that went wandering around. 'Ghosts' some people were calling them now, inspired by the title of the latest *Call of Duty* video game. And wasn't that the very area where drivers had spotted 'reddish things' hidden in the middle of the bushes? You only had to see the 'social media storms' online to understand the scale of the issue.

When one guy, who didn't talk much but drank a lot – which made the owner like him – had said to the old men, 'And you lot go to church on a Sunday to exchange the sign of peace . . .!' things almost got physical. Particularly since some of them had a 'red' past, from back when there was a party that really was a party, with leaders who came out and stood with the people. Real comrades! And priests, they didn't last long, for fuck's sake! Idiots!

In the end, there was a bit of a bust-up: between the owner, who had no intention of losing the best drinker, and payer, in the area; and the boys who, once in a while, felt the need to defend the views of the older men, who they still called 'crazy old dickheads', but who, that night, had got worked up arguing about family, shops, grandchildren who needed protecting and what was the best way to do that.

'Anyone who comes into my house won't leave alive. *Call of Duty: Infinite Warfare*,' Rambo concluded, crushing the can from the Coke he'd just knocked back like it was a neat whisky in a Wild West saloon.

Orso had muttered something very similar to himself that weird night of 2 November, as he kept pointing the rifle from one shadow to another in the shed. 'Anyone who breaks into my house won't be leaving alive.'

In a matter of seconds, Lupo had brought crashing down

everything that Orso had spent year after year piling up in the few square metres of the shed. A precarious but long-standing balancing act. It wasn't at all easy to move towards the back of the storeroom without the risk of tripping and falling. The moonlight, as much as its glow dominated the shiny black night, had no chance of getting between the tables secured to form compact, solid walls.

The situation remained unchanged for a good half an hour, with Lupo barking, slipping between the collapsed stacks and yelping loudly again, and Orso repeatedly saying, 'You're not getting out of here alive,' hunched over with the gun pointed at nothing in particular.

Suddenly, something happened that Orso couldn't explain.

The shed door slammed, as if caught in a fierce gust of wind, even though there wasn't a hint of a breeze that night. Lupo turned round, launching himself at him, seeming to go for his throat. That's how Orso almost killed the dog. Only a moment before squeezing the trigger, he realised that Lupo was attacking something that must be behind him – no, outside in the yard, on the other side of the door.

He turned round quickly, twisting at the waist, keeping his legs firmly planted on the ground, and in the middle of the darkness, he saw a very small black figure, carved out of the crystal-clear night. It stood, petrified, in front of Lupo, who was howling, ready to tear it to pieces.

With the rifle aimed and his finger on the trigger, Orso followed the dog out of the shed, while the creature clumsily put its hands on its head, covered its eyes and protected itself by leaning to one side, quivering.

29

Rome, 3 November – 8 December

The first thing Khaled had realised about the tunnel near what he called 'the Grand Station' was that this was a place where the police never show up, except when a tourist complains about being robbed. The whole matter is resolved with some hoopla that takes a few hours and a few detentions. In the worst-case scenario, one of the boys disappears for a bit. But they always come back.

Cross-eyed Omar, the boy the young worker had left him with, before taking off for who knows where, had already been through this twice. He hadn't picked up that purple crescent moon under his right eye in prison, no. But he had slept there, eaten there and even played a few games of football in the courtyard.

'Better than being here, believe me!'

He'd taken that punch in a house built specifically for people like him, and if they take him back there, he swears he'll burn the place to the ground, starting with the guy who when he arrived said, 'Welcome,' and proceeded to beat him up. 'Just so you and me understand each other from the off,' he warned. But Omar didn't give a shit. He waited two days for the right moment, and escaped again. If he ever sees that bastard, he swears he'll kill him. He slides a fingernail across his neck, mimicking slitting his throat. 'Loss of consciousness in five seconds, death in twelve,' he says. At least he'd be back sleeping in prison for the rest of his life, and that would be that.

Khaled still hasn't ventured onto the platforms, where he would be among the people coming and going from the Grand Station. To him, that stuff is like something from another planet.

Either he stays in the tunnel, looking at the scraps of paper Padre Buono gave him, figuring out how to continue his journey, or he crouches in a small flower bed under a tree that seems to bend in the wind, even though there isn't a hint of a breeze.

That this crowded space is just one part of a vast area, he'd understood when Omar, who can sort of speak his language and sort of make himself understood with gestures, told him, 'Tonight we're sleeping in the warm, eh? You, me and Red.' He'd smiled, pointing at the suitcase as if it was one of them. Khaled had liked that.

It had happened straight after the Great Fear, when a whole night of rain had brought sludge sliding down from the back of the tunnel. He doesn't know if it was the stench that woke him, so foul that it was attacking his brain, or the screams of the other boys who were trampling each other to get out, while the water spurted from the closed grate. If they didn't all get out, and quickly, they'd end up drowned, like the cockroaches they found floating upside down in the water the following day.

He'd seen people die like that, trapped.

On the patrol boat that had pulled them on board moments before the dinghy went down in a whirl, something like that had happened. Not because of the water, but because of the fire. Roasted in the engines. He could tell from the stench of flesh and the heart-rending screams coming from the engine bay seconds after some of the men had got inside, kicking and punching people out of the way because they were so freezing cold. The warmest place on the boat. They all crammed in there so they wouldn't die. Nadir must have heard them, too, even though he pressed his palms over his ears, the way he'd seen his mother do once in the courtyard when his uncle was slaughtering a lamb.

Now he thinks that, if he has to die too one day, he wants to die in silence, not in the midst of screaming: that's the thing that, for a while, has terrified him the most when he starts to think about death.

For a couple of nights, all the boys had had to fend for themselves, after the Great Fear.

He would never have imagined that so many of them would have the same idea as Omar. The driver just stuck to driving, watching the road, as if there was nothing and no one on his bus, not even the bittersweet stink of alcohol, sodden rags and slurry.

Sitting next to Omar, who'd slipped into the seat beside him, resting his head on his shoulder and his feet on the suitcase, Khaled hadn't closed an eye.

He could feel his breath on his neck. He turned to look at Omar from time to time when he twitched, opening his eyes wider than ever, on alert, and then letting his head drop back down. The rest of the time, Khaled looked out of the window, watching the city go by, opening out into squares, streets, roundabouts: a vast stretch of gold and, suspended above it, the night.

It seemed magical to him, the unexpected, and continued, appearance of colossal stones, planted there in a time so distant that Khaled couldn't even calculate their age.

There was even a moment when he ended up hallucinating. The tiredness had gone to his head. He imagined he was on a ghost bus, a corpse among corpses, slipped on board to stink up a seat while the golden city they were gradually passing through was being resuscitated; from the depths of the Earth sprang forth columns, statues, fountains, walls. He imagined that this was its way of breathing, one huge breath that would eventually swallow up everything – bus and corpses travelling along through the night – if a pink glow, turning orange, hadn't cast a strip of light onto the city's skin, stirring it awake.

'Time to get off. The ride's over!'

The driver's voice took him by surprise. Even Omar jumped, raising his head. 'S'up dickhead!' he shouted in a bastardised language all his own. 'The language of God,' he often joked. 'God wot speaks all languages of Earth.'

'Oh, thanks for the pillow!' he said, turning back to Khaled, slapping him on the back.

'All out the back door,' the driver shouted, pulling on the handbrake.

And so the belly of the bus set about emptying its bowels – bags, rags, stench – unloading its bunches of nocturnal passengers back in the open space that Khaled no longer found in the least bit impressive. Even the Grand Station seemed, all things considered, a place like any other at this grey hour when the lights on the huge building, 'the typewriter' some of the boys called it, had gone out and the day was not yet quite day.

But that was the night that Khaled had started to think of Omar as 'a friend'.

That's why he trusted Omar when Omar told him that whatever shit he had in his red suitcase, either he should keep it hidden in the tunnel or take it with him to walk around the station, without making himself too conspicuous.

30

Brussels, 20 December

For days, Karolina has existed in a state of constant frustration. She's still glued to the chat window with no signs of activity. No, 'Hello,' no, 'All okay here, Mama,' like the last time words popped up on the screen.

She hasn't given any more thought to the business from a couple of weeks ago, with the receipt and the lottery, not since she dropped her phone into her bag, annoyed with how curtly the woman from the discount store had ended the conversation.

Now it's almost Christmas and the market is back in Place Sainte-Catherine, with the little chalets brimming with mulled wine, kebabs, sausages, candy apples . . . even the carousel seems candied – aeroplanes, seahorses, ships, spinning to the sound of a lullaby, along with everything else (the colourful presents decorating the stalls, the people crowding to buy them, the tree and its cascade of lights and the majestic Ferris wheel dominating the skyline). Now that the world around her had filled, in the space of a few days, with an overwhelming, contagious happiness, Karolina had a real longing to speak to Fenna, to walk around with her, eating caramelised nuts and waffles with mountains of chocolate on top. Just wandering around the chalets looking for a present for Fenna might bring her some relief. But no. She even found herself envying that glassy but still bold look in the eyes of the fish sold in the market on beds of shining ice. She ended up buying two: one for herself and one for everything she's missing. But she never cooked them. She kept them in the fridge and, when the skin and eyes lost their shine and turned into a pale, deathly presence, she threw them out with the food waste, holding her nose.

The story about the red creature, the boy armed with a dagger or who knows what, and the two lorry drivers involved, had remained front-page news, especially in the tabloids and social media, until it was overtaken by estimates of Christmas spending. But the search never stopped. New reports, witness statements and evidence (like the discovery of a tatty pair of trainers not far from the motorway) played their part in identifying a possible link between the two events. The Brussels Capital police had been working on the case for weeks, with a thousand crossed wires to complicate matters. Detailed and discreet work, that's what the superintendent of the Brussels West Police Department had asked for. One way or another, he was determined to catch the kid that someone had said arrived on a coach from the south that is the source of all nightmares – while other people said the opposite, that he'd crossed the border, yes, but going the other way. Regardless of the direction, the superintendent from Brussels West wanted to catch him and look the little bastard right in the eye, hoping to get that vision out of his head. He still couldn't explain it, and one of these nights it might come back, with its little red suitcase and its brown skin, and attack him. That scared him, being attacked in his own home, even though, on that ridiculous night at the end of October when he'd kept vigil in front of the television, not a hair on his head had been touched, and everything in the living room had stayed, frozen, exactly where it was. Nothing more, nothing less, except for that little bastard's eyes; specifically that they didn't move a millimetre, they were so stubborn and sparkling . . . Maybe it was because they'd stayed wide open, staring at him, never closing, at least not until he'd allowed his own eyelids to drop for a few minutes. When he'd reopened them, there was nothing but the black screen. He found that sudden disappearance just as baffling.

The last thing the superintendent had imagined was that their search would lead to an identical line of nice suburban houses in one of the quietest, most respectable parts of Brussels.

There is a slight stench of rotting fish coming from the dustbin when the two police officers arrive at the address they were given by investigators at the discount store.

They look for the name on the doorbell, but Karolina had removed the label after the last visit from the police, when her potato-head of an ex-husband took the liberty of humiliating her, spewing his contempt, while she lay curled up on the bed with her eyes shut tight, hoping with every fibre of her being that Andreas would come back just in time to throw him out of the house.

'There is no Mrs Van Damme,' she wants to tell these two boys, who had simply read the details that the salesperson had copied onto the form from Karolina's documents, which still show, due an error that was never corrected, both her surnames, maiden and married.

She, too, can smell the foul fishy odour outside the front door, so she says, 'Do come in,' without giving it too much thought, when these two boys, who seem decent enough, explain that they've come about the receipt she's supposed to have saved.

At first, she takes a deeply embarrassed 'I'm sorry' approach. She's sorry she doesn't have anything to offer them, no biscuits or chocolates. She's sorry she still hasn't had time to put up a nice Christmas tree, sort out some lights in the front garden. And as she says this, she is actually sorry that she let them into her house, which seems even more bare now, in the middle of the festively decorated houses and lawns.

Only when one of the men carefully pulls a badge from his jacket pocket does Karolina realise how hasty she was to let these two into her home without asking exactly what they wanted from her.

Since she doesn't understand what the federal police might have to do with the discount store lottery, she bites her lip to keep herself from asking all the questions she wants to ask. She'd been waiting for that moment for months: a policeman comes to her house and says, 'We know where he is,' or, 'Come with us. We'll take you to your son.'

Her bag, with her wallet and the receipt in it, is in the last place she wishes she'd left it: in Andreas's room, by the computer. As soon as she got home, she'd gone straight to check the chat window. She was typing yet another message that would be met with silence when she heard the knock at the door.

So now that the policeman is asking her to please go and get the receipt, she feels a sudden surge of panic.

She's angry that Fenna hadn't insisted, months ago, that she leave the computer in her basement, where it would have been safe. This is the nonsense going through her mind as she says, 'Yes, I'll be right back with my bag,' moving tentatively and turning round to check no one's following her.

She would do anything – scream, swear, get herself arrested – to stop these two taking away the last little thing she has left of her son. It's the chat she's thinking about, the contact that she has learned to think of as enough, even when she's gripped by fears that she's talking to an imposter.

EVELINA SANTANGELO

'Here we go,' she says, sitting on the edge of a chair, in the hope that these two will be on their way soon. Fresh-faced. Too fresh, she thinks, afraid that they're here to play cat and mouse.

'Could you get the suitcase as well, please?' the other officer asks politely.

'What do you mean?'

In a flash, she thinks about the things she's heard on the bus, on the metro, and doesn't know what to say. All she remembers is a very old woman, wearing a lot of make-up, with two huge ruby-red earrings hanging from her saggy earlobes, and a disturbingly fleshy Botoxed mouth, turning to what must have been her husband, the pastiest man Karolina had ever seen, saying, 'If you ask me, all of them arriving from who knows where to do who knows what, they're like blood-sucking vampires, devilish. And anyone who says, "Poor things," I'd string them up one by one.'

'Why . . . the suitcase?' Karolina checks, just before the policeman can say anything, unable to stop her voice from shaking.

132

31

Po valley, Emilia-Romagna, 2–3 November

Orso had kicked Lupo out of the way, making him yelp. Then, with the gun still trained on the creature, he'd gently shoved it towards the house.

This failure to follow the golden rule, which the old man had never broken and which dictates that everyone should be where they belong – blacks with blacks, yellows with yellows, whites with whites, Christians with Christians, and beasts with beasts – meant that Lupo could take advantage of the opportunity to slip inside. While Orso carefully closed the door behind him, without taking his eyes off the creature, Lupo curled up by the fire, pricking an ear now and again, as if he was waiting for the shouting that, sooner or later, would chase him out to his kennel.

'Stay there!' Orso's voice thundered as he turned on the lamp on the kitchen table, only for it to explode into sizzling darkness.

'Fucking hell!' the old man yelled, as the room was plunged into the dim reddish glow of flames dying in the embers.

With one hand still on the light switch and the other steadying the gun against his chest, Orso wasn't shouting at Lupo, but at that creature, still holding its hands up. He could make out the tiny profile in the shadows stretching out into a dark corner.

'Face the wall!'

Orso groped around for the chair by the table and pulled it towards him, so he could position himself somewhere that enabled him to monitor the situation, and even have some support for the gun and his arms.

'Turn around!' he shouted.

The creature didn't turn. Nor had it lowered its hands. It was standing against the wall, swaying gently from side to side, when Lupo jumped to his feet again, growling.

'Down! I told you!' Orso shouted again, pointing the gun at Lupo, who looked like a red devil, his fur even shaggier than normal. Lupo flattened himself to the ground and disappeared against the dark floor, keeping his ears down to avoid being seen.

By now, the flames were licking high in the fire, and the dark shape of the creature seemed possessed by heat, a flash of reddish shadows that scampered up and down.

'Bastards!' Orso pointed the barrel at the creature again, ready to fire a bullet straight into it. Only a log landing with a thud in the middle of the ashes and turning the fire back into smaller, more regular flames put him off. What he could see drawn on the wall was nothing but a black shape: two long, thin sticks on a little ball that looked like a head.

If that thing had been a grown man, he would have already been done for. One shot, gone. That's what Orso had thought, regretting not having fired immediately, while it was sneaking around in the shed, like a mouse that you kill, but which always pops back up, followed by any number of other mice.

He'd ended up spending the whole night sitting at the kitchen table. The last time he'd done that was when he kept vigil over his ashen wife in the bed in their room, unable to find a moment's peace. He could see half of her lifeless body through the bedroom door, which he'd left open. He couldn't believe she'd gone like that, in her sleep. Without a word. The next day, his face was hard, like someone who'd never shed a tear. At least that's what people said. And he was happy to let them think whatever they wanted.

He had the pistol on the table and the rifle pointed at the creature, convinced that sooner or later it would collapse on the floor, or at least relax its arms, or whatever the hell they were. He really wanted to see how long it could bear standing there against the wall.

'And you, stay there! Stay!' he kept ordering Lupo, every time the dog tried to stand up, resurfacing from the floor, until he got up slowly onto his stumpy legs and, moving cautiously, belly to the floor, he howled so loudly that Orso got the message.

'Go and pee, and come back!' he said, opening the door, without shifting his gaze or lowering the rifle barrel.

'Let's see what kind of dough you're made of ...' he said, nodding. 'I want to know!'

The dough the creature was made of had to be very hard because, even though it was standing on those two stick legs, it wasn't giving in. Even its thin arms were tough, up above its head.

'I'll shoot you! Understand, shitface?' Orso had started to shout, exasperated, by the time dawn started to break outside, a pale dawn that made things in the room less shadowy.

'Watch that!' he shouted at the dog. In the hearth, the fire had reduced to a small heap of reddish ash. Lupo, reinvigorated by a liberating run through the fresh snow, got straight up and went to sit behind the creature, which tensed its shoulders.

Outside, the snow was thick. It was still falling when Orso

went out to load wood into the wheelbarrow. He had trouble pushing it back to the house under the leaden sky, bending over to alleviate the pain in his back. Old age punching below the belt.

Then he came back in, throwing open the door, and the timid light of day invaded some of the darkness.

In the feeble glow that filtered in from the doorway to the back wall, the creature was turning round, with its hands still up over its head.

'Fucking hell!'

Orso saw what was in front of him as if for the first time.

Letting flurries of snow turn the kitchen floor white, he sat down again at the table and started to watch the creature: its face smeared with something that looked like mud, like a black line of tar dripping down from its forehead, between its eyes; the knotty arms sprouting from the sleeves of a light shirt; bare legs, shivering under a pair of shorts. Bare feet, too.

Orso banged his fist down on the table.

Lupo flattened himself to the floor, quivering.

'You, stay there and keep guard!' he ordered the dog. A moment later, he'd bundled himself into the lined leather jacket that made him look even bigger and fatter, and slammed the door behind him.

Screeching off furiously and leaving a deep furrow in the snow, he pulled out into the main road, almost killing a guy trudging through the cold on a bicycle. The neighbour's fir tree, with its lights now off, was reduced to a gaunt silhouette in the fog, and he barely even noticed it.

'Give me three cartons of milk and a jar of honey,' he croaked at the grocer, scanning the street on the edge of town. He didn't want to bump into anyone. That's why he'd gone to that out-of-the-way shop, whose only customers were Romanian builders buying beer and sandwiches, and a few old ladies who'd always gone there to buy their essentials – they didn't need all that stuff from the supermarket, where you just got confused. 'The pre-war grocer's' was what most people called it, in a slightly condescending tone.

'I've got eucalyptus honey too,' the grocer said, pointing to his neck.

Orso cleared his throat. He almost spat the catarrh that came up onto the floor.

'I don't need that.'

'I've got a nice cotechino sausage in, as well.'

'Lentils will do me fine,' he replied.

32

Rome, 20–21 December

'If you don't go outside, you don't eat,' Omar had suddenly announced, after more than a month of bringing a slice of pizza or a sandwich down into the tunnel for him. 'Always out of respect for my friend,' he explained every time, referring to the young worker who brought Khaled to the Grand Station after they'd escaped the apartment that stank of glue.

Rather than ask people for money, Khaled preferred stealing. He had done it a few times. At the supermarket, where no one noticed if anything went missing. You just had to make sure you didn't get caught between the tills and the exit.

Once, though, when he was still with his brother, Nadir, he'd taken a big risk. He can't remember where they were exactly. Those places all look the same. Same aisles. Same neon light like a fever in your eyes: you look at all the stuff piled up in columns and it feels like it's falling on top of you. He's always liked the idea that there was a place where everyone could take whatever they wanted. As he stuffed packets into his coat, he never really thought of it as stealing.

Right after Nadir died, he'd had a dream that he died too, but in one of those supermarkets, in the middle of the lights, with boxes of biscuits, cartons of milk, bars of chocolate jumping off the shelves until they buried him.

If he hadn't started screaming like a slaughtered lamb that time the security guard picked him up and kicked him out, who knows how it would have ended. Nadir was watching him from behind a hedge. He couldn't leave him there: that was all Khaled could think, as the guard emptied out his trouser pockets. He almost pulled him down, grabbing hold of his arm.

He couldn't understand what was being shouted by the girl with the brightly coloured headband, as people passed by in a hurry to get away. But the guard certainly went red in the face. And in the end, he let him go.

'Before you go in, think about how to get out,' he'd joked later with Nadir.

'If you don't go outside, you don't eat,' Omar said again, offering to keep an eye on the suitcase in the tunnel.

But since he'd decided to do a tour of the Grand Station, Khaled would prefer to take it with him.

'Do what you want,' Omar said, nodding casually, then going with him to show where he could find a bite to eat: either in the bins along the platforms where people threw away all sorts, or 'There,' he pointed to a kiosk. Then he gave him a demonstration. He waited until the girl at the till was busy and simply stuck out a hand on the way past, then headed through the exit with an arm raised, as if to say, 'See you later.'

'Never stay still, especially if you're pulling something like that around a station,' Omar warned him.

So now Khaled walks, moving from one platform to another. From time to time he takes a look in the bins swollen with paper and cartons.

If his mother could see him, she would surely die of shame.

It's better to drink, fill his belly that way, he thinks, heading towards a drinking fountain. He does a quick about-turn when he sees two men in blue uniforms walking around, scanning the crowd.

With his heart beating wildly, he forces himself to walk indifferently towards the exit, which he can't find for the mass of people all going faster than him, in every direction. He doesn't know how best to go unnoticed: if he should rush too, or move slowly, taking care to avoid the CCTV cameras.

When he goes back to the tunnel, he hasn't eaten, or drunk a drop of water, for hours. He presses the palms of his hands against his eyes. He can feel the burn of some sort of tears.

If he hadn't made his mother that promise about Nadir, if he hadn't told her he would never abandon him, he would surely have gone back across the border and back to Padre Buono, who had always warned him about everything: what to do if they came to do checks on the building site, what to say if anyone stopped him in the street.

'I-am-a-minor and I-am-here-alone,' that's all he had to say, just that.

'So, did you eat?'

Omar's voice catches him by surprise while he's using his finger nails to clean bird poo off the shell of the suitcase.

He nods, tentatively.

Omar has a wonky smile on his face, even more wonky than his eyes. He pulls a pink pill out of his pocket. 'Take it!' he says. 'Good shit. MDMA. Trust me!'

After a moment's hesitation, Khaled snaps it up hungrily.

'That's right,' Omar says, swallowing one himself. 'Now go,' he shouts, pointing the way out of the tunnel, while Khaled stays sitting it the same place. 'Go, dickhead! Go!'

*

Dragging the suitcase behind him, Khaled goes back to the Grand Station, which is even scarier now that it's bathed in its colossal spaceship light.

This time, he does what he has to, with a determination he would never have imagined. He steals a sandwich from the kiosk. He steals a cake from a child who dropped it on the table when he went to join his mother paying at the till. From a man who's running for a train, zigzagging through the crowd, he steals a wallet. He pulls out the money, and throws the rest on the floor in the middle of the platform. He steals a can of Coke from a woman sleeping under a pile of rags. Taking care to dodge policemen, cameras and ticket inspectors, he dives into the crowd, coming and going, ready to pull the scissors from his pocket and jab them into the stomach of anyone who tries to stop him.

He only freezes when he spots Omar walking down the platform looking tense, like he's waiting for a train. Khaled heads over to meet him, to tell him, 'I've eaten!' Maybe even get a slap on the back.

'Get lost!' Omar says, as soon as Khaled is close enough, casting glances down the platform to where there's a man leaning against a wall, staring at them.

'You have to go! Got it?' He shoves Khaled so hard he almost falls over. Then he walks off. With his hands in his pockets and a baseball cap pulled down over his eyes, he follows the man, who's walking a metre in front.

Whatever is going on between Omar and this guy with a jacket, tie and briefcase, who reminds him of the surveyor Padre Buono used to chat to on the site, Khaled can't explain it.

What concerned him was the fierce look Omar had given him, a moment before he was swallowed up into the labyrinths of the Grand Station, his cross-eyed pupils scarily dilated.

*

When Omar gets back that night, he doesn't greet anyone. He crouches in a corner. He rips back the steaming plastic from a whole chicken. Using his hands, he tears off the meat and swallows it hungrily, without offering any to anyone. Then he licks his fingers and pulls a couple of banknotes out of his pocket.

'Don't look at me like that, faggot! Don't look at me!' With unexpected violence, he throws the money into a little boy's face. He lunges at him. He seems intent on beating him to death, even though the boy hasn't said a word. When he finishes blowing off steam, he straightens his baseball cap. 'Because if there's a faggot in here . . .' he starts squaring up to them all, one by one, driving them out of the shadows where they're huddled. 'That's you,' he says, pointing to someone at random, and goes back to scrutinising the others. 'See this? I earned this,' he snaps, collecting up the notes that have landed in a puddle of sludge and rolling them back up. 'Goodnight, I'm tired.' Slouching against the tunnel wall, he falls asleep with his hands stuffed in his pockets.

It must be really late when Khaled wakes up the next day, his head as heavy as a rock. There's no one in the tunnel, except Omar. Standing up, his hands still in his pockets, he shifts his gaze from the suitcase to Khaled, and back again. Then he grabs him by the collar. He lands a punch that makes Khaled's nose bleed.

'Asshole!' he screams, throwing himself at Khaled again, and letting go only to unleash an even harder kick against the suitcase, which topples over.

Getting to his feet and pulling the scissors from his pocket takes Khaled a matter of seconds. Then he strikes out with the blade, at the height of Omar's throat. Omar dodges the blow and throws Khaled to the ground again, strangling him.

'If you move, I'll end you!' Omar shouts, holding him down

with his entire body weight. Then he leans closer to his ear: 'So you think you can go around with this thing, no worries, and nobody will see you? That you're invisible? You dickhead!' Leaving Khaled stunned on the ground, he wraps the suitcase in a blanket.

Khaled wipes away the blood streaming from his nose, and looks at him, clueless.

'A dickhead and a total asshole!' Omar says, dropping the suitcase into his arms. 'Now walk! Before they come looking for you!'

He goes to give him a shove, wrapping his fingers around his neck.

Outside, the streets around the Grand Station are full of people and patrol cars, circling around like hunting dogs. A police van has even appeared outside the main entrance.

Ducking round the corners of buildings and dashing forward, Omar warily gets to where he needs to be.

'Now, you and this thing stay here!' he says, diving into an underground rathole that stinks of sewage.

'And don't even think about going out in that blue coat. Wear the other one,' he orders, pointing at the jacket from the discount store. 'This one here,' he says again, holding it up to show him and pretending to put it on. 'And I'm a dickhead, too, getting myself in the middle of this mess,' he mumbles to himself, as he makes his way back to the surface, leaving Khaled there among the thick cobwebs and spiders dangling in the pitch black.

33

Palermo, 21 December

If Inspector Vitale had avoided his usual round-up of internet news that morning, he could have saved himself from ruining his whole upcoming Christmas. The fact that the branches on the Christmas tree outside the police station, on the other side of the fence, didn't have a single bauble left, had already got him wound up.

'It's always them. The regulars,' Officer Genovesi noted, referring to the kids who, every year, descended from the 'neighbourhoods' to sweep everything up. The 'neighbourhoods', in the officer's jargon, generally meant the city's galaxy of derelict suburbs.

There's no point looking at the stills from the CCTV cameras at the entrance. Because They, the fathers, grandfathers, uncles, or whoever 'They' are, always send out the youngest kids – just five, maybe seven years old – as scouts.

Last time Inspector Vitale had gone all the way out there, just to make it clear that, next time, no one would be getting away with it, they just looked him up and down like he was a raving idiot. When Genovesi ironically said, 'So, what? It was these ghosts?' someone actually considered it.

'Why? Couldn't it be? Anything's possible in this world.'

'It's just children messing around! Kids' stuff!' one woman

interrupted. And she said it in a voice that was so sweet that Inspector Vitale didn't even know how to reply.

The video he'd had on his computer screen for the last quarter of an hour was not high resolution. It had been taken on a CCTV camera set up on a pillar at a station. A few minutes in which, in wide and dizzying spaces, you could see the flattened, almost two-dimensional figure of a boy wearing a bluish coat, and behind him a suitcase that, in those grainy images, seems to move by itself. It's hard to make out any facial features, even in freezeframe. He could tell it was a boy by how slight he looked. The brown complexion suggested he'd come from somewhere south. But boys like that were ten a penny round these parts. Distinguishing them from the boys 'off the boats' wasn't easy.

IF YOU SEE THIS MINOR, INFORM THE POLICE IMMEDIATELY, said the writing scrolling along the bottom of the screen.

It wasn't the news itself that caught the inspector's attention but the jerky, unnatural movements and two-dimensionality emphasised by the very low resolution of the video. The way that, at one point, the figure disappeared altogether, exiting the mechanical eye's field of vision, which brought to mind the last thing the inspector wanted to remember: nonsense that it was best to archive and have done with, without spending too much time thinking about it. But he's been forced to think about difficult things for months, since the incident with the identikits and everything that followed: delusional reports, mothers and fathers who wanted their drowned children back, phone calls from other sectors, and the boy perched in the living room piercing him with those eyes, which some mornings had attacked him again while he was half asleep, making him leap out of bed.

His painstaking daily task of cover-up and erasure was helped by two strategies that he had encouraged in the investigation.

'Low profile' and 'no fuss' was the line the Sicilian authorities had agreed with the editors of national and local newspapers. When it came to social media, they were relying on boredom. They certainly couldn't keep on frightening people, especially not with Christmas coming and everything that meant: crowded streets, presents to buy, shopkeepers who could finally breathe a sigh of relief.

Even the headteacher – after the intoxication of interviews, statements and articles – ended up welcoming a suggestion from Maestra Iolanda, who felt the all-too-heavy weight of responsibility.

During a class council meeting with no shortage of tension, drawing from the depths of her despair, Maestra Iolanda had rattled off a list of questions and answers that were compellingly logical, in their way. Disguising the tremor in her voice hadn't been easy.

'Do these children exist?' she began. 'Maybe they do, maybe they don't.' She answered her own question, shifting from one side of the argument to the other.

'So, these children are practically invisible, or only visible in their own way ...' she added, almost tripping herself up. 'So, let's say they don't exist, and have done with it.'

What she did next was so unexpected that everyone in the room was genuinely stunned. She took the drawings, which had been returned to her, out of a folder and started tearing them into tiny pieces.

Her sigh of relief, when she looked at the meaningless pile of grey confetti at her feet, finally broke the room into unanimous and liberating chatter.

What worried Inspector Vitale more than a little was the idea that thousands, even millions, of users could resurrect those ghostly images reproduced from CCTV footage of the station in the capital, and that the defence chief might ring him again ...

That's why, in the end, he decided to close the page.

'All we need is some mother, father, grandparent, or sibling showing up to claim this one, too.' He said it in a way that he intended to sound ironically creepy. Then he grabbed the jacket hanging twisted on the hook, and went outside to get some fresh air.

34

Brussels, 24 December

The last thing she'd imagined was that she'd be spending Christmas Eve in a police station.

Her statements hadn't convinced the officers who came to her house on the pretence of talking about the lottery. She didn't know how to explain the whereabouts of the suitcase that she'd bought a few months earlier, and she contradicted herself multiple times. At first she denied everything. She couldn't remember buying anything like that. 'Maybe a shopping trolley?' she ventured, when they persisted. 'And definitely not red,' she protested. There wasn't a single red thing in her house. She hated red, if they really must know. But then, faced with the evidence, she caved. She said that, yes, maybe she had bought it as a gift for her friend Fenna. But then she hadn't done anything with it, 'because it was faulty,' she added, remembering the story about the buckle that she'd been told by the girl on the phone.

Only in the end did Karolina confess. Yes, she had bought the red suitcase for a boy who needed it.

'What boy?'

'A boy . . .'

'And you didn't wonder why?'

'What was I supposed to wonder, sorry?'

'What he needed it for. Because that wasn't just any boy,' the other officer said, without knowing quite what else to add.

'He seemed like just any boy to me,' she said in her defence. A rage was bubbling up inside her, which had to have something to do with Andreas, who those officers didn't seem to know anything about. Not a mention, not a reference, as though she didn't have a son of her own to find.

'Why would I care about that boy!' she exclaimed, contradicting herself yet again. 'He was frozen. I bought him some biscuits, something ... I can't remember exactly. I was there. He was there. And I bought something for him.'

'A red suitcase,' one of the two pressed.

'A little case where he could keep his stuff dry. It was cold. It was raining.'

'It wasn't raining that day, madam!'

'I haven't done anything wrong!' She sounded desperate now.

'That probably wasn't your intention. But ...'

'Then what's the problem? I don't understand! What's he got up to, with that suitcase? What has he done?' she finally asked, in a voice that was almost talking about her son.

A question that the officer didn't really know how to answer, to be honest.

'The problem is what *he could still get up to now*.' The other intervened, to put an end to this back and forth that was creating problems, so many problems, given that neither of the two knew exactly why the superintendent of the Brussels West Police Department was insisting on this investigation.

Sitting on a chair in an empty room, Karolina has been waiting a good half an hour for someone to explain why they called her in there.

'Good evening.' A man's voice behind her, kind in its own way, catches her by surprise. 'Merry Christmas, first of all.'

That cordial tone makes her even more nervous.

'I know. You probably have much better things to be doing . . .' the detective says, as if he's trying to apologise.

'I have a guest for dinner,' Karolina lies, in the hope that they'll let her go.

'I see. We won't keep you long,' the detective says, sitting at the desk. 'Now, a few months ago, you bought a red suitcase for a boy you met in a discount store.'

'I didn't meet any boy,' Karolina insists.

'Do you usually buy suitcases for boys you don't know?' asks the detective, half serious, half sarcastic.

'It was just chance. I don't know why I did it. He asked me and I bought it for him.'

'So, he asked you for it . . . And why did he ask you specifically, madam?'

Karolina looks at him. 'Because I was there,' she says.

'There were a lot of other people there, I assume.'

'It was just chance,' Karolina says again.

'Do you at least remember what this boy looked like? What kind of face he had?'

'I had other things to worry about.'

'What worries, madam?'

Maybe she should tell him about Andreas, go on the counter-attack. She was owed some explanations herself, after all!

'I was thinking about my son who disappeared,' she murmurs.

'I'm sorry,' the detective says. 'I'm sorry you lost your son.'

Karolina doesn't know whether to correct his mistake or let the policeman think whatever he likes. Maybe he's only pretending not to know. That thought confuses her even more. It all seems so absurd. Being there, in that room, to give a statement . . . about nothing. Then she shudders. She remembers her bewildering journey through the propaganda sites, the horror of which has come back to her again and again, and it scares her.

'Anyway, what do you want from me? I haven't done ... I mean, I bought a suitcase. I could just as easily not have done. It happened. I have no idea about anything! If he stuffed it full of dynamite ... If he hid severed heads in there ... I don't know anything! I didn't see anything! I lost my son. I wasn't myself! Do you know what that means, *to lose a son*?' After spending months in a kind of lethargy, waiting, these words pile up with a desperation that surprises even Karolina herself. 'I'm sorry, I'm not myself,' she mumbles again, drying the tears she didn't want to cry, not there, in front of a stranger.

The detective passes her a tissue. 'I'm sorry, madam. What we want to know is whether you remember his face,' he explains, trying to de-escalate. 'That's for starters. Because, from what we know, you met this boy *by chance* at least a couple of times. And so, for now, we're trying to take things one step at a time.' He says it like he's talking to a child. 'So now you're going to come with me to a different room and give me a hand, okay?'

'Don't tell them anything!' her ex-husband had advised, referring to Andreas. When she'd called to ask him to go with her, his only response had been 'No chance,' followed by a long rant against, 'those dickheads ... who only know how to screw things up, even just for a fine ... Fuck them all! Don't say anything!'

Karolina is thrown by this, too, as she mechanically gets up to follow the police officer, who has already said more than he intended.

The other room is even more bare. There's just one seat in front of a window; on the other side is a white wall.

'Now, look carefully and try to remember.'

Karolina looks, as ordered, waiting for something to happen. Then she opens her eyes wide, turns to the police officer, and then to stare at the features of the boy who has appeared through the glass: a thin figure that looks like it's been drawn on the wall, staring into space. He probably doesn't know that anyone's watching.

'What do I need to do, sorry . . .?' she mumbles.

'Look carefully. See if you recognise anyone,' the detective says, without taking his eyes off the figures filing by one after the other. Same lost stares. Same scruffy hair, as if they'd all just been pulled out of bed. Many of them bundled into acetate tracksuits that are too big for them. Some wearing trousers scrounged from who knows where. Each of them stands with his back against the wall for a couple of minutes, then in profile they walk back to the side where they first appeared, passing like a shadow over the soundproof glass.

'Do you recognise anyone?' the detective asks after a while, breaking the silence Karolina has sunk into.

She presses the palms of her hands against her eyelids. She looks again at the boy with his back to the wall, scanning the room, confused. He's not much more than a baby.

'How many suitcases did that discount store sell . . .?' she blurts out at last, with a kind of nervous laugh.

'Think about your answers, please, madam!' the detective huffs. 'Is that boy one of *these*?'

Karolina shakes her head.

'Did that boy look like any of *these*? Madam, I asked you a question!' the detective shouts, when Karolina goes to stand up, determined not to answer anything else.

'I want to get out of here! I want to go home.'

'Then you're refusing to cooperate . . .'

She doesn't respond to that particular point, but her refusal is very clear.

35

Po valley, Emilia-Romagna, 3 November – 24 December

Orso didn't get it. For weeks he'd left the bowl of milk and the honey on the floor, near the wall where the creature was still standing, unfazed. He'd pushed the dish up to its bare feet using a stick he always kept within arm's reach. He'd waited a bit to see whether the creature would bend down to take it. To begin with it had never changed position, but a few days ago it had lowered its arms to its sides, although Orso hadn't seen when that happened. But the rest of the time, it hadn't moved. At least not when he was in the house. So it still wasn't clear who was emptying the bowl. He had a suspicion it was Lupo. He was now lying by the fire almost all the time, keeping guard. The only thing Orso was sure of was that, despite the greasy black clumps mussing up its face, the thing's complexion was less pale. But the ends of its fingers were still black from the cold.

'Maybe it's fine as it is . . .' Orso mumbled to himself after he'd uselessly decided to throw it a blanket, which, in the end, Lupo had settled himself down on. 'Fuck it, then!' he yelled, annoyed with himself. It wasn't like him to be soft. Offering it milk was bad enough. After the first time he'd kept repeating this gesture of holding out the dish for it every day, morning and night. 'Like an idiot,' he'd let slip, in one of his solitary chats with old Lupo.

'They don't make cats like they used to!' he'd complained, that night, which was in fact Christmas Eve, as he came back from the shed into the house. The glue spread on the cardboard had done its work. The mouse was stuck to it. Somehow, picking it up and throwing it away was the only part Orso found disgusting, his only weakness, and he'd hoped that some cat would have done his job for him. Instead, the mouse was still there, squirming. There was nothing else for it. Orso loaded his hunting rifle and prepared to squander a cartridge to finish it off. To destroy it and not have to think any more about it. When he went back inside, he took it out on Lupo. 'They don't make dogs like they used to either!' he said, spitting on the floor.

When Lupo just raised one ear in reply, and let it drop again, the creature stretched its face into a smile, revealing teeth, which were small: milk teeth.

That was how Orso came to realise that this thing that had turned up in his shed was actually a child. Lupo must have realised, too. He brought the blanket that had ended up on the floor close to the creature's bare feet, and settled himself there to sleep, enjoying the heat of the fire on his nose, no longer keeping guard over anything.

The uproar around the country had completely escaped Orso. He only went out to buy essentials. The rest of the time he stayed at home. And he didn't even consider going to the bar.

The story about the boy with the red suitcase was now on everyone's mind. Many people had decided to stop sending their kids to school two days before the Christmas holidays. At the comprehensive that had seen the most protests about the unresolved issue of the 'illegals' – bearing in mind that these schools 'accommodated' children from the Roma camp in much higher numbers these days – the headteacher had given his word: from the new year, no one would be able to come and go as they pleased. Surveillance cameras at the entrances and in the gym, he'd explained in the speech he gave to parents before the holidays.

'And in the meantime, they're happily wandering around our stations. There could be anything in that suitcase: guns, dynamite. Let's just hope they're not planning on throwing us a big Christmas party,' the local secretary of the most popular party in the Po valley region wrote on Facebook, below a video of the little boy in the blue coat, voicing the concerns of his fellow citizens.

'There'll be no need for CCTV cameras round here,' one of the guys from the bar assured his younger brother, on the morning he was due to start his 'rounds', according to the rota drawn up by Rambo and the others.

The last leg was Orso's house.

'What do you want?' That's how the old man welcomes him on Christmas Eve, leaving him outside, in front of the half-open door. Rifle at hand, barrel to the ground, hands on the stock, as if it were a walking stick.

'It's fucking freezing. Let me in, yeah?'

'That's your problem.'

Jigging around in the snow to warm himself up a little, he does what he came to do. He gives the little speech he's reeled out several times this morning, to warn the locals.

'On New Year's Eve, I don't recommend going out.'

'Says who?'

'No one in particular. But we don't recommend it,' he suggests again.

'What do you mean? Listen here,' Orso says, in the tone of someone who certainly doesn't let anyone tell him what to do, lifting the rifle to his shoulder with practised familiarity.

'This is just what I'm telling you, and a dozen other people,' the kid replies, watchful, as Orso lowers the gun. 'For people living in this area, near the motorway, it's better to stay at home on New Year's Eve.'

Orso takes only a second to pull the rifle back out of the snow that has piled up in front of the house and point it at the guy's belly. 'Get lost,' he says.

'Hey!' he says, jumping back with hands in the air, tripping over a semi-submerged log. 'Oi, I warned you!'

'Get lost, shitface. I fucking mean it, otherwise . . .' Orso leans over, pressing his eye up to the sight.

'It's for your own good. Stay shut up in the house, you old dick.' But the guy only comes out with this line once he's at a safe distance. The fact that Orso can't hear him inspires even more colourful language that he would never have dared utter in front of any of the older men. You never know with those old boys!

'Cocksucking old bastard,' he says, raising his middle finger in the snow, once he's out of Orso's sight.

'Bunch of junkie bastards.' Ever since the morning, Orso has continued this diatribe against Rambo and his pals.

He stays angry with everyone until the evening. With the lentils that take an eternity to cook properly, and with whoever grows them – they're such poor quality now, it's daylight robbery. With Lupo, using his old age as an excuse to lounge around like a lizard – he doesn't even bark when some dickhead turns up at the door. With the neighbour's intermittently fucked-up fir tree, and with the clear night that makes those lights perfectly visible in the dark, even a whole kilometre away. With his wife who's not there, and hasn't been visiting him in his dreams. With the mice that are still not extinct. And with that thing . . .

By the time he's moved on to a nasty diatribe against the child, he's already on his sixth glass and has only just put the lentil soup on the table. A plate for himself, one bowl for Lupo, 'And another one for that,' he says, shoving it over to the wall, 'and Merry Christmas to all!'

The fact that Lupo laps up the broth and spits out the lentils riles him up even more. He's drunk an entire bottle of Lambrusco and opened another. The only reason he doesn't give the dog a kick in the ribs is because it's Christmas Eve and 'We've all been good,' he slurs, raising his glass. When the child apparently doesn't like it either, and, crouched down on the floor, seems to be in cahoots with Lupo, Orso reaches the end of his tether. 'This is how it works here! You eat what there is!' he says. But his words come out wrong, the way they only ever do when he's having a solitary chat with Lupo, when he's thinking that this animal is the only thing he cares about, at the end of the day. Since he's been on his own.

So, the last thing he could have imagined, that Christmas Eve, was that he might end up picking up his rifle again and pointing it at the child.

36

Rome, 24 December

Omar hasn't shown his face since last night and now Khaled's stomach has started eating itself. He's got the feeling that there's something very wrong with his gut. Staying down there, in the dark, is making him feel worse. The stub of a candle that Omar left him has shrunk down to a lump of deformed wax.

For the last few hours, to pass the time, he's been telling himself the story that his mother, Leila, had always told Nadir to send him to sleep: the little spider who was king of all the spiders in the world. Why? Because even though it was a tiny little thing, it was far more cunning and intelligent than all the other spiders who were fat, freakish, foolish, feverish, fiendish ... and at that point, Nadir wouldn't stop laughing. He'd laugh with his belly, his face, his eyes, even his teeth laughed.

Khaled, on the other hand, is on fire everywhere: his stomach, but also his throat. He can't stand another minute buried down there. He puts on the jacket the woman at the discount store gave him, following Omar's advice, even though it's tattered now, and goes outside.

It's the first time in months he's gone anywhere without pulling the suitcase behind him. At first it makes him uncomfortable. He feels defenceless.

He stuffs his hands in his pockets against the cold. Pulling down the cap that Omar left him, walking close to the sides of buildings, he heads towards the station, intent on rummaging through the bins along the platforms. He's sure to find something. He has no idea that it's Christmas Eve. He can just sense a strange atmosphere, an electricity in the air. People in the street carrying dozens of parcels and packages. A good sign, he thinks. Perhaps he'll find plenty to eat in the bins, too.

He's so happy to be back in the open air that, after a while, he almost enjoys the cold. As he walks quickly, he starts to feel like singing. So he does. The words to a song he used to sing at school come into his head. 'Ta, ta ... tu, tu ... ti, ti ... I'm the letter t. You'll find me in words like tamr, teen, tuffah ...' He's still following the happy beat of this little song about the letter t, when he finds himself in front of a giant fir tree at the station entrance. He'd really like to take any one of the packages piled for decoration under the branches laden with coloured baubles. Take it and open it, just like that, for the fun of it. He's distracted by his stomach clenching. He's so hungry that if he thinks about it, he feels faint.

'Ta, ta ... tu, tu ... ti, ti ... I'm the letter t. You'll find me in words like tamr, dates; teen, figs; tuffah, apples ...' He keeps walking, peering into the bins. He would throw everything up in the air, toss it all onto the floor to make it faster, take the best scraps and bite into them, if he didn't have Omar's words in mind: 'If anyone out there recognises you, you're dead, got it?' He pulls the cap further down on his head. He quickly grabs half a sandwich that's sticking out from the top of a green bin. He drinks water from the fountain.

That it's late evening, he can tell from the station clock. It must be the din on the platform, the brakes that seem to whinny, the voices on the loudspeakers running one after the other, but if he had the suitcase with him, he's sure he would hop into any old carriage and get away as quickly as possible. He's staring at the end of the platforms, where the station lights end and the trains set off into the dark, when he realises a man is looking at him.

He turns round quickly, heading for the exit. At first, he doesn't run. He walks very slowly, to avoid getting noticed. Then he hears a voice behind him. 'Hey, you!' It's closer than he thought. Now he, too, sets off like a train, but towards the glaring lights of the station entrance. He loses his hat. He loses the other half of a sandwich he'd managed to scrounge. His mind is blank with fear. At last, he disappears round a corner.

Just then, the guy freezes, looking around anxiously. He's twisting the boy's hat in his hands.

'It was you … I'd swear,' he says to himself, thinking of the boy he saw in the video a few days earlier, 900 kilometres away from here. Leaving the island to take a few days' holiday in Viterbo with an old friend from officer training school, and get certain stubborn thoughts out of his mind, wasn't a bad idea. With his bag over his shoulder, Inspector Vitale goes back to the platform. The train to Viterbo is about to leave. There's no sense in missing it. In fact, all that would do is make things even more complicated. As he puts his foot on the first step, he looks back one more time, mechanically. 'It's better this way,' he tells himself.

Khaled finds the right street by instinct. He just waits until there's no one around, then slides down into the cobweb-infested depths where he left his suitcase, and where he is met by dim candlelight.

There's no breath in his throat to call out for Omar, to check it's him in there. As he goes down, he can smell the stench of dead mice.

As soon as he gets close enough to the light source, his legs almost give way. Horrified, he can't move. Omar looks horrified, too, in the candle flame that distorts the lines of his face.

'What have you done?' The words explode in his mind in a roar, but Khaled's voice comes out so quietly when the words actually leave his lips.

Omar jumps to his feet. 'Are you crazy? Crazy fuck!' he yells, as Khaled pounces on him. If the scissors were within reach, he'd slit his throat. Instead, all he can do is punch him in the face. He hears his teeth cracking under his knuckles. The blood running from Omar's nose and staining his hands sets him off even more. Only when he sees him motionless on the ground does he stop. Behind Omar's head is a little patch of blood.

Shaking, Khaled goes over to the dark corner where Omar has left his suitcase lying open. What he can make out, as he gets closer, reminds him of two red lips, open; in the middle, some sort of giant greying worm, the strips he'd seen Padre Buono busying himself with in the hut after the accident, while he stood petrified against the wall.

He closes the two shells of the suitcase, gripped by nausea. He can't hold down the vomit in the bittersweet stench that has invaded this sewer deep below street level.

'I'm here, Nadir ... I-am-here-Nadir,' he starts to murmur, rocking back and forth, back and forth, a never-ending lament.

This lament is still going on, albeit much more faintly, when Omar regains his senses. With some difficulty, he stands up. He dabs the wound on the back of his head with a rag and his nose with the sleeve of his coat. Then he turns to Khaled. He watches his torso rocking like a pendulum.

'What are you doing with that ...' he can't even say what he's seen, and not because he doesn't know the word for it, '... in there,' he finally slurs through broken teeth and bleeding gums, pointing at the suitcase that is back standing in the dark.

Khaled looks up, still unable to stop rocking.

'My little brother,' he murmurs. Then he stands up, and puts his few belongings into the blanket he'd wrapped himself in on the nights he'd slept down there. Now he just wants to get away, to carry on with his journey.

37

Po valley, Emilia-Romagna, 24–25 December

The last thing Orso could have imagined, that Christmas Eve, was that he might end up picking up his rifle again and pointing it at the child. Suddenly and for no reason, the creature's eyes had widened. Thrashing around, it started yelling, chanting verses in a language that only the Devil himself . . . Lupo was on his feet, too, growling, as the demonic thing grabbed the bowl of lentils and hurled it into the middle of the room.

'Stay there! I'll shoot you! Stay there!' Orso grabbed the rifle resting against the door. Standing up in such a rush sent the alcohol straight to his head. Everything started to spin and he fell to the floor. Face down, he pulled the rifle over to him, while the creature walked towards him, one step at a time, with Lupo launching himself at its bare calves, unable to sink his teeth in.

When Orso took aim and fired, the child was gone. He couldn't tell if he'd hit it. As if in a dream, he saw it dive out of the door, with Lupo close behind.

It took him a while to get up off the floor, clinging on to the table.

Staring deep into the clear night, staggering, he focused on following Lupo's tracks in the snow.

'Come back here, you bastard! If I get hold of you, I'll skin you alive,' he mumbled to himself, venturing into the blue darkness that stretched over the Roma camps and the road.

He didn't know how far he'd wandered into the middle of nowhere, with fresh snowflakes slowly covering each track.

'Come back here . . . I'll skin you alive!'

At some point, in the grip of the drink that was clouding his brain, he was afraid that Lupo was lost forever, or that that thing had taken him away to who knows where.

It was almost dawn when he spied a pile of fur in the first gloom of day. Stumbling, his legs heavy, he set off in that direction, propping himself up with the rifle.

He must have rubbed his eyes several times to make sure that really was his Lupo, curled up beside the child, which seemed to be sleeping in the middle of the deep snow, or maybe it had passed out, and Lupo was licking its face, as if he was trying to wake it, or warm it up.

Slinging the rifle onto his back, and bending down to pick up first Lupo and then the child was instinctive.

He didn't know whether it was the cold he'd been exposed to all night, but he couldn't feel his arms on the way home.

There was pure white silence all around. For just one second, Orso got the feeling that some kind of wild animal was following them. He imagined eyes peeping at him. But when he turned round, behind him there was only a vast expanse of snow, and above it, suspended, a veil of fog. Nothing else.

38

Brussels, 29–31 December

She knows they could have tapped her mobile phone. And she can't be sure they're not spying on the computer, too, but she can't get by without logging on for at least a few minutes. Just enough time to check the chat.

She's convinced that if she can just be very quick, she'll be able to get round any monitoring.

In the chat window she finds an empty message. She goes to shut everything down when she realises there's an attachment. She opens it. On the screen, a kind of digital card appears, written in an elegant font.

A special New Year's Eve. Music and fights. Mixed martial arts meetings. The finest warriors in Europe. The best bands. 31 December. Start 18.30. Moerbrugge.

The street address is on a satellite map that Karolina downloads onto the computer along with the invitation. Then she leaves the page. She opens the website of the bank where she has her almost-empty current account. She makes a transfer for the ticket price, following the instructions to the letter.

New Year's Eve is in two days. She can get by without turning on the computer again until then. She's sure nothing else will happen in the chat in the next few hours. Knowing she might have a way to meet the kid who calls her Mama, who she's been in touch with for weeks, and maybe even speak to him, makes her feel better.

'They can find him by themselves, that boy with the suitcase!' she says, trying not to think about anything else.

When her ex-husband decides to call her for news, she treats him with disdain. 'It's better if we avoid contact,' she says. 'You might end up in trouble.'

The last day of the year begins with a light drizzle that doesn't stop all morning.

She'd bought the train ticket to Moerbrugge the day before, after cleaning at the agency, where she'd found another woman dressed in the same uniform, with the firm's golden logo stitched more or less over the heart.

'Good morning. My name is Saliha. I'm on a trial period,' the woman told her when she got spooked walking in.

'Finally, they've realised I can't do everything by myself,' she replied, trying to hide her jitters. Only the manners of the woman, who spoke politely but with a strong foreign accent, and seemed to be out of her depth, encouraged Karolina to explain what she had to do. And besides, she had other things on her mind that day.

Of all the direct trains to Ostend, which stop in Moerbrugge, she'd chosen the 16.25. An hour and half's journey and she'd be there.

And that's how it went. By 17.55, she was in the small Flemish town. All according to her carefully planned schedule, as if the success of the whole night depended on those details.

When Karolina arrives at the venue, there's nobody outside. For a moment, she worries she's got the wrong street. With the invitation in her hand, she's still unsure about looking inside. There's a bouncer in a leather jacket, standing with his legs spread at the entrance, who calls over to her: 'If you're here for the rally, come in – everyone's inside.' She just has to give him her name and fill out a form. 'A formality, to avoid nasty surprises. Troublemakers,' he adds, very politely, as if he were talking to his mother, or grandmother. 'Welcome!' he says at last, pulling back a green curtain, beyond which Karolina finds herself between two giant totem poles with writing on that she doesn't stop to read.

She hadn't thought there would be so many people inside. Boys, mainly, some girls. All very young, and very tattooed.

On a banner that dominates what seems to be a large gym, NATIONALISTS AGAINST GLOBALISATION is written in capital letters in the middle of the back wall, between a stage and some kind of large cage with a platform inside.

It's not that Karolina feels completely at ease, quite the opposite, but being surrounded by kids chatting, drinking from plastic cups, and wandering between the benches, waiting for the evening to begin, makes her happy. She thinks this is a nice way of being together. She's surprised when she asks for a beer and a boy in a black top and jeans tells her they don't serve alcohol. 'Only at midnight, for a toast,' he explains, pointing to the bottles of bubbly arranged in a corner. Karolina opts for a lemonade and starts to scan the room. On the front benches she spots piles of cyclostyle copies and roughly printed publications. She doesn't read those either. She concentrates on the kids, who seem like they own the place, hoping to spot a face that recognises her as the woman from the chat.

She must seem happy, because someone catches her eye and gives her a nod of acceptance, surprised but inexplicably pleased that this woman of a certain age, wearing a yellow raincoat, should be there with them that night.

After a while, the lights suddenly go down and everyone turns to face the stage.

A guy with bulging muscles takes the microphone.

'Welcome!' he shouts, prompting an enthusiastic cheer.

'Tonight, we are honoured to have with us the best bands in Europe. From the Netherlands, France, Germany, Italy, England, Wallonia and as far afield as Flanders,' he jokes, raising approving laughter. 'Meanwhile, over there,' he says, pointing at the cage, there will be displays from the best MMA fighters, also joining us from every corner of our Europe.' At these words, a cheer goes up in the room. 'On the other hand, we're all warriors, revolutionaries in battle!' the guy goes on, drawing more applause and a loud roar of 'Yes!' He makes his way across the stage and points his finger at someone in the crowd. 'Among us tonight, we have a special guest from Germany.'

Karolina doesn't know who this guy Axel Reitz is that everyone's looking around trying to catch a glimpse of. When he steps onto the stage for a moment, she realises he's a very different kid to the others. He seems staid and is very formally dressed. He is the only person there in a jacket and tie. His thin, rectangular spectacles make him look professorial.

'I'm here to support my Flemish friends,' he says. Later, he'll give a speech he's prepared for the occasion. 'When the time is right,' he adds, disappearing back into the middle of the audience, who are now chanting his name, even though to Karolina he just seems like a grey figure. 'A pale German,' she thinks.

Then, after a moment of total darkness and bated breath, all hell breaks loose. The striking of a chord on an electric guitar followed by ear-splitting drums. It's not this that troubles Karolina, though. She'd almost been expecting it. It's what happens in the cage and around her that she hadn't anticipated, not to mention her reaction.

Now the crowd is one compact mass, cheering at every flying kick, every punch, the volleys of knees to the face that the fighters land on one another with a violence that makes her wince. Strangling, lever moves made with increasing force as the crowd cheer on the sculpted, tattooed, semi-naked bodies to go at it harder, and harder still. Even the music is mounting to a dizzying crescendo, with the bands taking turns, one after the other. Ultima Frontiera sing in Italian and the crowd sway. Karolina can make out just a few words: 'hope', 'loss' for those without tradition, and then the words 'welcome', 'dance', 'delusions', 'immigrants' ... When the Dutch group Brigade M come on stage, a roar erupts. The title of the song is 'Eigen Volk Eerst' – 'Our Own People First'. The kids start to shout, singing along, while in the cage, an eagle with outspread wings, sculpted onto the back of a fighter, launches itself in a flex of his dorsal muscles, and strikes down on a body knocked to the floor under the gaze of the referee, who raises his arm. He confirms the victory to the sound of screamed lyrics about people falling into the abyss, racial mixing that stabs at the heart, holy wars, Islam and Judaism.

It's at the halfway point of the evening that the pale German, Axel Reitz, reappears onstage, clearing his throat to make his speech.

'Today, we are not here to fight for money or to get rich,' he says. 'We're here today to fight for the generations to come. To keep Europe as the continent of the white race. We're fighting, not just for ourselves, our families, our people, but for the thousands of years of Aryan culture we share! We're fighting for a system where every population is a nation. A system based on blood, soil, identity, culture and race. We're fighting for a new world order, comrades!'

Karolina is immersed in a jungle of raised arms, when a girl in a T-shirt with BOMBS 88 printed across the chest, and runic victory symbols tattooed on her wrists, grabs hold of her elbow. 'Arm up, comrade!' she says with a laugh, and then, with a violence that knocks Karolina sideways, 'Lift that fucking arm, comrade!'

'Hammerskins forever, forever Hammerskins!' she hears her chant. 'Blood and Honour!'

Karolina only realises that she's started shouting and trying to shield herself, while the girl rages on about her fucking arm stuffed into that ridiculous yellow raincoat, when one of the security guards pulls her out of the swaying mass of stretched bodies and takes her to the door, saying something in her ear that sounds like the 'Mama' that had brought her there in the first place.

The last words she sees before she finds herself back on the pavement are on a sign that says AGAINST GLOBALISATION. WORK AND SOCIAL JUSTICE FOR OUR PEOPLE.

39

Po valley, Emilia-Romagna, 31 December

The flames start to rise from the camp at exactly midnight, when Orso has just popped open one of his bottles of Lambrusco. One glass for him and one for his wife. He does it every new year. His tradition. Even though his Cesira never touched a drop in her life.

It's not that he's alone, but he may as well be. The child has been asleep for an hour now, curled up beside Lupo, who hasn't moved a muscle. Now and again he pricks an ear, like he's monitoring the situation.

Just an hour ago, the boys had left the bar, screeching onto the icy road. They'd had a few drinks, snorted a few lines. They'd had a blast. Some of them had had the bright idea of bringing their girlfriends along, even though Rambo had told them to keep themselves free. So the first problem was how to get rid of the girls, who couldn't wait to go dancing at Mammut, the coolest place in the valley. With the excuse of going to top up supplies of the good shit for the rest of the night, they dropped the girls at Lele's place. Half an hour, three quarters at the most, and then they'd be back. There were a fair few bottles in the fridge, Lele promised, saying goodbye to his girlfriend, who was slightly miffed by this sudden change of plan.

When they arrived at the camp, the lines they'd sniffed had taken effect, the vodka too. But they followed Rambo's orders to the letter, while two of them kept watch on the street. There was nobody around at the camp, bar a stray dog that didn't even have time to bark, Lele was so quick to lasso it and slip a plastic bag over its head. Arranging the kindling at strategic points was easier than they'd expected. The smell of petrol spilled like piss went to some of the boys' heads. They didn't seem to laugh so much as bray while they soaked the wood.

The rest happened in complete silence. Rambo took the Zippo from his pocket and lit the first pile of sticks, giving the green light to the other fire starters.

Crackling and sizzling sounds, then the first flame, nice and high, followed by more. 'Happy New Year, *rats!*' they choursed, their faces flushed, once the fire had started to do its work.

Three quarters of an hour precisely. Lele's calculation had been spot on, Rambo congratulated him as they arrived back at the house, blaring their horns to let the girls know.

Once again this year, Orso makes a toast, chinking his own glass against his wife's, resting on the kitchen table. 'To health!' He drinks, then he downs the second glass, too, just as he'd always done, every year since they got married. His arm is still in mid-air when, through the window, he sees the darkness in the distance turn red, and then colours like some kind of Northern Lights have been switched on across the white fields. He spots the high flames a few moments later. He might have stood to watch the spectacle, if he hadn't been struck by one particular thought.

He closes the shutters, pulls the curtains. Approaching the child carefully, so as not to frighten him, he wakes Lupo, who jumps to his feet, in turn waking the child. 'Come here.' He motions for the child to come closer. 'Who knows what might get into the heads of these . . .' he mumbles, as he slowly reaches for his gun. The way he says, 'Don't worry,' and the gesture he makes to go with it must be deeply convincing, because the child doesn't run away, even if, for a second, he squeezes his eyes closed and shrinks into his shoulders, gripped by fear.

Orso doesn't really know whether what he's doing makes sense. But it's the only thing that comes to mind, so he does it.

'Now, look,' he says. He picks up the rifle and shows the child how to handle it.

He pulls out one of the cartridges he always keeps in his pocket. He sits down and rests the stock on his left knee. Then he places the cartridge in the loading flap from the pellet side. With his thumb, he pushes the shell into the chamber until he hears the sound. 'Click,' he says to make the child under-stand. He repeats these same movements until it's fully loaded. Holding down the action release button on the lock, he pumps the slide back and forth. 'Come here,' he says, going over to the door. He fires a shot into the middle of the night and it burns red. He pumps the slide back and forth again to expel the used cartridge. He pulls back the hammer and inserts a cartridge in the loading flap.

He repeats this process all night. At least the child will know what to do, if anyone comes while he's not there. With that thought, the next morning, he prepares the bowl of milk, even though the child seems to be sound asleep, and who knows when he'll wake up?

What the boys spot at dawn, hiding in the woods by the motor-way and the camp after their wild night, is a veil of black smoke rising slowly from the carcasses of caravans and skeletons of cars. In the middle of it all, they can just make out groups of men, women and lots of children wandering around, lost and ragged. They're too far away, though, to hear their cries and lamentations.

After their night at Mammut, Lele's girlfriend wouldn't hear of going home, but in the end she gets sick of waiting in the car for the boys to come back. 'Still out there pissing?' she shouts, walking into the woods. 'But . . . What happened? Who was it?' she asks, turning pale, completely ignorant of it all.

'How would we know? Who knows what they keep in there, in those shacks . . .' says Rambo, jumping in before Lele can say anything. 'All we know is that none of *them* can hide in there any more,' he adds, referring to the story about the 'illegals'.

'Hey, shall we make a move? Before we freeze to death,' Lele says, warily, patting Rambo on the back.

'Yeah, let's go. Since there's nothing left to see,' he confirms, clapping his hands together to shake off the snow.

THIS IS JUST THE BEGINNING OF THE END, RATS! written in spray paint welcomes in the new year on a wall not far from the 'pre-war grocer's'. Rambo had wanted to paint one corner with the symbol of Wolf of the Ring, the gym where he'd been training until recently. Loyalty and Action.

The first to see the enormous black graffiti are the Romanian builders, who pass by on their way to work on the building site. This morning they brought sandwiches and beer from home, seeing as it's New Year's Day and the grocer's will be closed, like the rest of the country, still sleeping, peaceful and white.

40

Rome to Naples, 22 January 2021

The car Khaled is travelling in is the kind you only see in films. The pearl grey of its bodywork shines in the early-afternoon sun. He's never felt a seat like this, one that cradles him like a giant hand emanating heat. Between the music that permeates every corner of the car's interior and that gentle rocking – even though they must be going really fast, judging by the speed of trees and cars whizzing past the window – Khaled releases tension that hasn't left him for days. He doesn't sleep, but it's like he's dreaming a restorative dream. For the first time in months, he feels safe. Invincible.

The idea for him to continue his journey by car, rather than in some train carriage, had been Omar's. His way of apologising for what he'd done. How could he ever have known . . .? He'd promised his friend that nothing would happen to Khaled, so now he has to keep his word. This is how he convinced him to agree to travel with a stranger, even though he had no idea who he was or what he did for a living.

'I've got him by the balls,' Omar said, and Khaled realised it was the guy from the station who Omar had been walking behind that day he came back to the tunnel with a whole chicken and a ton of cash in his pocket. 'Trust me,' he assured him, resting a hand on his back. 'Omar knows what he's doing.'

The suitcase had been put in the boot, underneath the felt upholstery, near the spare wheel. Then the guy placed several suitcases on top, all much nicer than his. Black, leather.

'He's a big shot,' was the last piece of information Omar gave Khaled. Maybe that's why he's had his sunglasses on ever since they set off, Khaled thinks, and why he's never turned to look at him or say anything. He drives, he watches the road, now and then he exchanges a few words with a faint voice that comes in through an earpiece. All things considered, Khaled quite likes travelling with someone who seems like a secret agent.

Omar had wanted to celebrate the decision. On New Year's Eve, he'd come back to 'their basement', as Khaled calls it now, with a couple of bottles of very cold, very fizzy beer. He opened them with the tip of a knife and wanted to make a toast, slamming their bottles together. 'Even though you nearly battered me to death!' he added, letting out a big laugh, as if he needed to free himself from a thought, some private torment.

That was the time he confided in Khaled about his plans.

'I'm changing my life,' he told him. 'And I'm gonna change it for all these bastards, too,' he added, referring in general to the people in the street above their heads. For once, he hadn't given him one of those enigmatic, sarcastic smiles. Khaled couldn't really understand what he was talking about, but he raised his bottle in a silent toast. 'You're going south and, me, I'm heading north,' he went on, half smiling now. 'Belgium. All expenses paid. Big money, eh? They're expecting me. So fuck it!' He made a gesture that indicated something dramatic. For a moment, the muscles in his face froze. 'Because, let me tell you. People are alone,' he mumbled, lost in thought. 'I'm alone. You're alone. That faggot is alone ... all those dickheads up there are alone, when you think about it . . .' He nodded up to the street. At last he raised the bottle again. 'Oh, hey, we should organise a high-class party to celebrate together, the two of us!' He went out and bought another couple of beers.

He'd given him a big hug, before Khaled got into the car.

'Oh, look after the boy. Make sure he has everything he needs,' Omar whispered in his ear, nodding towards the suitcase. And even though Khaled didn't know the meaning of every word, he understood. It wasn't until later that he realised Omar had slipped a few hundred euro notes into his jacket pocket.

Khaled wants the last image of the person he now thinks of as his 'best friend' to stay in his mind, the way he'd seen him through the back window, as the car was pulling away. It came back to him several times during the journey: Omar wrapped up in his coat, hands in his pockets, bathed in sunlight. His eyes completely crossed. He didn't know whether he was looking at him, or the streets around him, to cover his back. He didn't move an inch as the car drove away and the shape of him got smaller and smaller until it shrank to nothing. Just then, Khaled got the impression he raised his hand, waving it in the air to make himself seen one last time.

The journey is shorter than Khaled expected. He's a bit disappointed.

He hadn't realised there was a sea crossing to reach the city that Padre Buono had circled in red on his piece of paper.

When it's time to enter the port, the guy signals to Khaled to jump in the back and hide on the floor, between the seats. A moment later, Khaled feels a blanket cover him. He tries to disappear even more, flattening himself against the bottom of the car.

His friend Omar had warned him that there would be a point where he needed to hide. He hadn't thought he'd be there all night, though, with the sound of chains and the uninterrupted purring of engines. The boat engines from the dreams of the old man in the city of glass mountains on the river.

That thought, the memory of telling stories in the warehouse (before the old guy ended up splattered when the windows exploded on his head), keeps him company during the crossing. At least he's warm and dry, and not afraid of dying, he thinks, recalling his last journey at sea, together with Nadir, and the corpses they had to step over to ask for help, to wave, so that they didn't die too, a lifetime ago.

41

Brussels, 1–15 January

Karolina has no idea how to get back on her feet. The only thing she can contemplate with any degree of lucidity is that she has lost everything. She doesn't understand how this could have happened; she can only acknowledge it. Dwelling on things won't do any good.

Just for a moment, when she got the news that came like a kick in the teeth, she'd thought back to that sign she'd seen as she was being escorted out of the venue on New Year's Eve in Moerbrugge. AGAINST GLOBALISATION. WORK AND SOCIAL JUSTICE FOR OUR PEOPLE.

She'd never thought that the words spoken onstage could apply to her personally.

'Who gets jobs? Who gets money? Who gets public housing? Who gets benefits? Who is treated with generosity in our country, comrades?'

In unison, the crowd chanted, 'Them! Immigrants!'

Perhaps if she went to those kids for help, someone would listen to her.

Although, for the last few days, she hasn't had the energy to think about things like that.

When she saw her photo in the paper, after the initial shock, a bitter smile had crept across her face and stuck there, fixing a sort of permanent mood. Even during the few hours she manages to sleep, she has the feeling that the smirk is still on her face. 'Possible sympathiser' she was labelled by the officious journalist.

She realised that this article was a new low as soon as she saw that the superintendent of the Brussels West Police Department had commented on the details of her case for the sake of one paragraph in the local rag.

She was sure her ex-husband would think it best not to get in touch. What she did expect was a phone call from Fenna, especially the day she heard the news.

She couldn't find any other way to account for what had happened to her, straight after that photo was published in the newspaper, where she looked like an ageing housewife with shifty eyes. Who knows when they took it. The kick in the teeth – she can't think of it any other way – came shortly after the Christmas holidays. One morning, she arrived at the agency at dawn and found the owner already there.

As far as she could recall, this had only happened on one other occasion in ten years. A period when the business must not have been doing too well. They'd had to carry out 'restructuring', make 'difficult staff cuts', she'd read when she peeked at a news-letter abandoned on one of the desks, instantly regretting giving in to her curiosity. Since she had the keys, she could go into the agency when there was no one there. It was a big responsibility, a show of trust in her. Stick to the job, know her place, that was the unwritten agreement that she had always respected. That was probably why she'd been there for ten years. It was also why she'd always done things properly at work.

She'd put a lot of effort into explaining the job to what she thought was going to be her 'right-hand woman': which products to use on the glass, how to get all the rings off the tables. So, that morning, she felt betrayed.

The words the owner had used to let her know that it would be best to reach a 'mutual resolution' were sharp. The conversation was brief, but with specific mention of 'recent events', and the 'unfortunate circumstances' she now found herself in. The owner had at least had the decency not to wave the newspaper under her nose. A copy was simply sitting on his desk and he made the entirely natural gesture of resting his hand on top of it.

In the end, Karolina signed, more out of fear of the owner moving this conversation into the open, where the other cleaning lady could hear, than because he'd convinced her. There was no need for any more humiliation.

'I hope ... that this is not ... because of me,' the woman mumbled in that very proper way she had, despite the very strong foreign accent, when Karolina picked up her things from the locker in reception. 'I'm sorry,' she added, looking genuinely mortified.

Karolina put on her coat and picked up her bag without a word.

'I have children,' the woman went on. The ridiculous thing was, she seemed scared.

'We all have children.'

Karolina didn't say anything else to the 'migrant', closing the door on her way out.

She hasn't turned the computer on again, not even out of curiosity or just to search the internet for news about herself, to read what people are saying. What would be the point, anyway? This *nothing* in which Karolina spends her days, waiting for the inevitable to happen – the day when, for example, the landlord turns up because she has no way of paying the rent – seems almost the best possible way to go on, the only way. The alternative would be to go back over it all, step by step, in an attempt to find a reason for everything, and lose the only certainty she has left: nothing that's happened to her makes any sense.

42

Po valley, Emilia-Romagna, 15 January

The official statement on the fire at the Roma camp, the party's local secretary had decided, should be issued as a tweet. He'd got a taste for it. He just had to type a small number of efficient words, without too much explaining, and, bingo: thousands of hearts. 'Who knows what they had in the caravans in that gypsy camp,' he wrote, and the phrase was repeated and amplified thousands of times in less than half an hour.

It read like Rambo had dictated it himself. This incident had given no small boost to his reputation among the boys as a visionary. No one dared to contradict him now, not even as a joke. Besides, there was a very serious matter to resolve, and quickly.

The tip-off was what anyone in the village would have called a 'bombshell'. The man who'd given it was someone they could depend on. 'Mr Christmas' the boys called him, because of his Christmas tree laden with increasingly psychedelic decorations, novelties ordered online from an American company where he'd worked as an émigré.

He claimed to have seen Orso stumbling around in the snow with his rifle on his back. At dawn. It may even have been Christmas Day, although he couldn't swear. What he was 100 per cent sure of was that the old man was holding, in his arms, a dead child. He'd said, 'Some kind of child,' because it wasn't like 'one of ours . . . A child that someone would look at and say: "Oh, that's a child."'

When he decided to tell this story at the bar, on an afternoon that seemed to be descending into the usual boredom, none of the older regulars wanted to believe it. 'Yeah, Orso's babysitting a kid now—' the owner of the bar said.

'A. Dead. Kid. Not alive. Were you listening or what?' interrupted Rambo, who had instantly put two and two together. Specifically the fact that the old man, on Christmas Eve no less, when Lele had gone to warn him about the 'New Year's Eve party', had left him freezing to death outside the door. 'Imagine if he'd dared let him in!' he said, in a huddle with his boys.

A while later, they were all at Rambo's house, shut up in his room plastered with posters: Stallone, Schwarzenegger, the legendary Bruce Lee, but also Chuck Norris. On the wall just above the bed, looking like a bolster, was written LOYALTY AND ACTION: WOLF OF THE RING, the organisation he'd been training with until recently. That he'd never managed, even in the most athletic years of his adolescence, to transform his belly into sculpted abs had always been his only regret. But baggy hoodies help. The most unusual thing about his bedroom is the arsenal he's collected over the years.

'Everyone has the right to defend themselves how they want, when they want, where they want. I'm with the people protecting their territory. Loyalty and respect.' His motto.

First of all, he had to distribute the right weapons to everyone. Into the hands of the one guy who knew a bit about these things, he placed a 20-gauge, which certainly couldn't dispatch a quantity of lead like the 12, but allowed him to see and position his shot better. The 22-gauge semi-automatic Colt he held out to another. 'Oh, I love this one!' Then he handed out the 28-, 32-, 36-gauges . . . For himself, he'd kept a .357 magnum revolver. He gave Lele a gun that fired blanks, but could still cause trouble. The knuckleduster he tossed to the biggest guy in the group, who caught it. He went on for a good half an hour distributing his 'creatures' and explaining what to do for everyone about to have their 'first time', the phrase drawing a nervous, braying laugh from them all.

'Magazine loaded. Slide. Now it's good to go. And shit gets real.' Lele paid particular attention to his meticulous actions and equally precise words, with admiration. 'You stay covered, always behind me!' Rambo told him, and he nodded an emphatic *yes*. You could tell from a mile away how scared he was.

They park the cars on an out-of-the-way street not far from the old man's house. They wait until it gets dark. Then they move out, keeping a certain distance apart so as not to attract attention. A dozen dark silhouettes spread out across the snow.

The yellow glow from the window, filtering through the drawn curtains, gives what little light they need.

'Let's do it!'

Keeping their backs to the wall, they encircle Orso's house. The plan is clear. First they peek inside, and then, with a well-aimed kick, they break down the door, 'like pastry' assured the carpenter in the group, who knew a thing or two about doors and locks.

It isn't Lupo who alerts Orso, but the child, who at one point begins to stare at the window as if hypnotised. 'Hide! Down!' Orso shouts at him, turning out all the lights.

The blanket the old man throws over the child, frozen stiff in the sudden darkness cast over the house, draws a little scream from Lele. He's just seen a giant black wing flapping inside the room.

'What the fuck are you doing?'

Lele can't explain. Half petrified, he falls back into position, following Rambo's orders.

There could be five, ten, or even twenty of them, Orso thinks when he spots a number of brown figures emerging and disappearing in the dark. Even the fire burning in the hearth is doing its bit. It magnifies shadows out of all proportion. So, for a moment, Orso doesn't know how to cover his back. He scans the room from one side to the other, while Lupo continues to doze, seeming to be somewhere else altogether. He doesn't even move when Orso tries to shift him with his foot. These things only happen when there are gypsies about, someone once told him. '*Those people* are brilliant at hypnotising dogs without anyone knowing.'

He has prepared the rifle and is putting a cartridge in the Beretta when, suddenly, he notices a frantic buzzing that seems to come straight out of the walls, then the crunch of steps crowding towards the front door.

'It's me or them,' he thinks, rushing across the room with the rifle pointed, and opens the door a second before Rambo can aim his kick.

Orso sees a crowd of spectres springing back in the snow and regrouping as a clump of heads and chests stuffed into padded jackets.

Recognising Rambo, standing in front of the others with his hands in his pockets, he starts to breathe again.

'So it's you . . .' he says, keeping the rifle up.

'We know everything,' Rambo replies.

'You need to fuck off.'

'Let us in.'

The old man simply moves the barrel of the rifle from one man to the next as he counts them.

Then Rambo gives Lele a signal. The shot doesn't launch into the air on cue, but when it explodes, it rumbles loudly in the dark.

'That clear?' Rambo says. 'I've waited months for this moment. To catch one and take it out. Killing one to teach a hundred,' he adds. He doesn't know where the quote comes from, but he thinks it sounds cool.

'Fuck off and play somewhere else,' Orso threatens, nodding in the direction of the Roma camp, now reduced to little more than a few charred skeletons.

'I think it's more fun to play inside,' says Rambo, who seems to have really studied his part. Then he points the revolver at the old man's face, like in a film. 'My patience has run out,' he says, giving the signal for the others to take out their weapons all at once.

A moment later, something happened that none of the boys would ever be able to explain, not even Rambo. The fact is that they had to run. No one ever dared say, 'Like rabbits.'

Shots were fired, that happened. Not one or two but a hail, a shower of bullets from every direction: the old man's house, the shed, even from behind them.

'What the fuck is going on?' Rambo had shouted, watching as the old man closed the door, without firing a single shot himself, as the bullets flew along unpredictable trajectories.

'How fucking many of them are there?' Lele ran as fast as he could away from the incessant fire, even though there wasn't a soul in sight.

When Rambo ordered the 'retreat', there was no one left behind him. Just the roar of engines and the screech of tyres.

'This isn't the end, old man!' Rambo yelled from his car window, firing into the air what was, in the end, the only shot he managed to take in the whole commotion.

If anyone had still been there, by the front door, when Orso decided to go back inside, they would have seen a tuft of hair poking out from behind the sofa and, on the coffee table so full of wormholes it was barely standing, Orso's Beretta still smoking.

'Well. Done. My. Boy,' the old man murmured, as if he were in a trance.

His mind went to his wife, to the son they never had. He reached out to put his hand on the child's head, but he dodged the touch, forcing Orso to pull back his arm.

The last words of that long night Orso directed at Lupo, who had finally decided to slink out of a dark corner, still shaking.

'Next time, we have to work on his aim.'

In all his years as a widower, no thought had ever made him so happy.

43

Palermo, 23 January

The island is bright. That's the first feeling Khaled gets when he leaves the belly of the ship and the darkness where he's spent hours shut inside the car, among dozens of other cars and lorries.

The exhaust fumes filtering through the air vents, while they were in line to leave the car deck, made him feel sick. Back on land, below the back seat, he felt every bump as the car left the metal plate for the quayside.

Now he's back in the front, with the window open and that orange light everywhere, he feels revived. He's sad when the guy presses the button to raise the blacked-out window.

He's hungry, he's thirsty and most of all he needs a really long wee. But he doesn't say anything. Maybe it won't be long until they arrive.

If it had been night time, maybe the port would have reminded him of something. That's where he'd arrived in a Norwegian vessel, after they'd been rescued by the coastguard's patrol boat.

If it had been night time, he'd have remembered precisely the two things he's never forgotten, from straight after the landing, after the black swirling of the sea, the screams, their names being yelled by two boys who were drowning, the corpses he'd stepped on to reach the arms of the people pulling them to safety, and the stench of flesh roasting in the engines, the cold, that cold that wouldn't go away as he and Nadir huddled under the gold paper they wrapped them in, like something from 'science fiction'.

And the things he's never forgotten, from straight after the landing, are the shadows cast on a cloth in a corner of the port – people 'off the boat' caught in the flash as they were photographed; and then the black cellophane stuck to the seats of the coach they eventually had to get on – after being handed a small bag with an apple, a sandwich and a bottle of water inside – to take them somewhere. They didn't know exactly where. 'Like lepers,' murmured someone who knew how these things worked, spitting on the carpet. 'Disgraceful, watch your manners,' his mother, Leila, would have tutted. She cared about these things; she said that respect begins with how you treat other people's stuff.

The cheese sandwich that the smart man, still so smart, hands him with a bottle of water seems like the best gift to start what could be the last day of his journey.

He watches the road slip by, still deserted, and takes huge bites of the sandwich. Then he crumples up the paper, looking for somewhere to put it. He's mortified when he sees the disaster of crumbs he's left all over the seat. He closes his legs to hide them. As soon as the man turns to look out of the window for a second, he brushes them all away with one quick swipe of his hand.

While it's highly unlikely that a secret agent wouldn't know where he was going, at first Khaled gets the impression that he is flying blind. He seems to be going round in circles. Hesitant, he takes the piece of paper from his pocket, the one where Padre Buono had written everything there was to know, once he arrived on the island. He's not happy that the guy doesn't even look at it, but he seems to have understood where to go. He turns down one street and drives quickly onto a wide, straight boulevard, one of those roads that know where they're going.

'Pee . . .' Khaled says, when he really can't hold it in any longer. 'Pee,' he says again, loud and clear, speaking one of the words he's learned in these months. There are a few others: 'I'm hungry', 'it's cold', 'beer', 'move it!', 'get in!', 'fuck off', 'dickhead', 'shit', 'station', 'south', 'sea', 'suitcase', 'red', 'my brother', and 'friend', the word cross-eyed Omar taught him when they toasted the journey he was about the resume.

This time, the guy looks at him from behind his sunglasses, and after a while, he pulls over.

Khaled doesn't understand why the guy is now leaning over towards him. He freezes against the backrest. But then he realises what's going on, and he relaxes. Stretching over towards the door handle, the guy is opening Khaled's window. He points to a shady spot in the middle of the trees. That's where he should go to pee.

He doesn't know how much is still trapped in there to come out. At one point, the endless stream of urine started to freak him out. He didn't even do it all. He just fastened his zip and that was it.

Too late. The guy had already taken the suitcase out of the boot.

Khaled didn't shout. He didn't yell at him to stop. He looked at the car sliding away, and the suitcase on the ground, unable to move a muscle. He couldn't believe he was leaving him here, on the side of this road where he couldn't even see a patch of sea.

Who knows what Omar would have to done to him if he'd been there.

If only he had a map . . . But he doesn't. He just has Padre Buono's piece of paper with a telephone number and a place circled in red. There's no telephone around here, though, and besides, he hasn't got any change to use one. So he walks.

'Who knows what the Good Lord has in store for us,' his grandmother, Samira, used to say. And as he repeats this, shaking his head, he knows he isn't expecting anything good.

Khaled follows the road, which narrows at one point, twists and then widens out into a long road that ends in an open space.

If there had been a wood on one side, and the motorway on the other, it would have reminded him of the lay-by where he'd slept in Brussels before he started his journey. Here, too, there are a few lorries parked and a lot of rubbish. Only here the trash is concentrated in one high pile, a stinking mountain, in the middle of waste from burnt-out bins.

The idea of finding himself back where he started is more disheartening than anything he's faced so far. He thought he'd made it.

Unsure what to do, he sits down. He takes the piece of paper from his pocket and starts to look at it, waiting for something to happen. But nothing happens. He stares at the paper, looks at the lay-by. Sniffs the air that stinks of burnt plastic.

The boys who pass by at some point are carrying a ball. If he could understand what they're saying, as they push one another around, bash each other and then laugh, he would at least know where he was: at the Clearing. The Northern Expansion Zone of the city where he'd landed.

The bricks positioned a certain distance apart, at two ends of what passes for a football pitch, the puddles on the ground, remind him of something very familiar, which he used to love before he left home. It's not as if he'd been a champion like his friend Hakan, but he knew how to defend his half of the pitch.

When one of the boys motions to him, as if to say, 'Come here!', he's almost tempted to get up and play. 'We need one more, come here!' the kid shouts. 'To play!' he persists, pretending to kick a ball. Then he tells him to fuck off because Khaled shakes his head. He stays sitting where he is, 'The spanner!'

He doesn't know how long the match lasts, with everyone yelling at each other, powerful shots crashing against the cars parked along the Clearing and against the dogs that get in the way.

When the boys tuck the ball under their arm and go their separate ways home, it's already dark. The air is warm, it doesn't seem like winter.

If at some point Khaled also moves from his spot, it's only because he can't stay there. That was made clear to him by the boys perched on the seats of polished motorbikes much bigger than they were. In a frightening roar of engines, they surrounded him. One of them lit a joint. 'Good shit. Home-grown,' he said, lifting his chin in the direction of a tower block, and letting out a chuckle.

'What the fuck are you telling him ... dickhead,' one of the other boys sniped.

'This kid doesn't understand shit. Can't you see, he doesn't understand shit ...' He looked around at the others. 'Here, smoke!' He put the lighter under Khaled's nose. 'Whoooom!' he went, mimicking a burst of flame. So, Khaled sprang up off the floor, and ran, with the suitcase in tow. He almost ended up in the middle of the rubbish. That made them all laugh. But they only laughed, they didn't follow him. That in itself felt like a miracle.

Now he's alone, exhausted and hopeless. He has no idea how far he's walked. He doesn't understand why he still hasn't reached the sea, if this is an island, the island he was supposed to get to.

*

Inspector Vitale spots him curled up on a bench under a tree. The suitcase is under his head, like an enormous pillow.

It's the middle of the night. He'd been working late. He's thinking about his morning arguments with the cleaning lady about burnt coffee; the insipid coffees he drinks in front of the machine at the police station; the piles of paperwork on his desk; the fights; the girl from the bar, who has no intention of accepting his invitation to dinner – she has other ambitions in life, that's what she told him; the loose change left in his pocket, now it's almost the end of the month . . . basically whether his lot, this half-life filled with nothing, hadn't, in fact, turned out to be everything he'd never wanted. He'd like to drop everything for at least a month, run away to an island, a real one. Sea, sky and not much land. Just enough. No one on his back. Not having to be the loyal police inspector. That's why he decided to take himself on a solitary walk: to get home as late as possible, enjoy the silence, the unusually warm night and even a bit of darkness, if only there weren't all these jaundiced street lights.

This is the mood he's in when he sees the twisted shape of the boy asleep, hugging the red suitcase.

It takes him a minute to work up the courage to put a hand on his shoulder. Just feeling flesh and bone against his fingers dissolves his fears. Then he thinks again. Maybe those two glasses of rum he had at the bar – the most Caribbean thing available – in an attempt to clear his head, have done their work, and now he's feeling something that isn't there. He presses his hand against the shoulder of the creature, still in a deep sleep.

He hadn't expected him to jump up, like a coiled spring, scrambling down from the bench, trying to escape.

Then he grabs hold of him properly, and picks him up. Fuck it if he kicks, just don't let him scream.

'You're okay now . . .' he whispers, trying to calm the boy.

44

Brussels, 23 January

Fenna's call came while she was standing in the queue. This was how she'd started saving. One euro for a hot meal. If one day she needs clothes, too, she knows she can find second-hand things there at a good price. For now, she can just rely on a limited wardrobe. That in itself seems like a blessing. She can even keep up with the rent for a while. A few months for sure. She doesn't want to think beyond that.

It hadn't been an easy step to take. From the first day, she'd taken care to sit with the people who looked most like her. There are quite a few, and she liked that. She'd hate anyone to think she didn't have a roof over her head. She still has a house, and she wants that to be quite clear. If she chooses her outfits more carefully than usual, it's because she knows how important appearances are. She's even gone back to giving herself a dash of eyeshadow and dab of lipstick. Someone who's temporarily hit hard times. That's what she wants them to think of her, the people who run the centre. Even the way she takes her plate, says thank you and then sits at the table is very polite. She doesn't smell, she doesn't wear rags, she isn't starving. She eats slowly and makes sure she clears everything away. When she stands up, it's as though there had never been anyone sitting in her seat. She's also careful about which stop she gets off at. She prefers to walk part of the way, changing her route. She wouldn't want anyone to see her.

She doesn't answer Fenna's call, which, if she's honest, she's been waiting for for months. That day the room is busier than usual and there's a constant hubbub. She's too embarrassed to explain herself. She's also afraid that someone will start shouting. That has happened once before. A vicious fight between two women who wanted to sit in the same place. One of the two insisted it was a disgrace, that she had booked that seat with the director personally.

When one of the workers pointed out, very politely, that everyone could sit wherever they wanted, the woman went so far as to pull a scribbled note from the pocket of her threadbare jacket. 'This is the proof that I'm right,' she announced. It wasn't easy to convince her. In the end they'd set a place at another table, at the back. 'The director sends his apologies,' said another worker, who seemed to have more experience. 'Today your reserved table is over there.' Only then did the woman back down, letting the worker show her to her place.

'If we start with that, stealing people's places . . . that's it! We're done for!' she muttered.

Karolina is back outside, in the street, when Fenna calls her again. This time she answers on the first ring. No hard feelings, she promises herself, as she says, 'Sorry, it was a bad time . . . I didn't pick up quickly enough,' her tone studied. Aloof but not hostile.

Fenna doesn't beat around the bush. She doesn't apologise, doesn't feel the need to explain herself, as if there hadn't been those months of silence between them. 'How are you? Are you in trouble?'

'Yes,' Karolina replies, making an assumption about what her friend is referring to. There's no point in denying it.

'I'm sorry.'

She's pleased to hear her say something sensible at last. So she gets straight to the point, too. 'They're saying things . . .' she tries to explain, but she can't go on.

'I read it.'

'Listen, I didn't do anything.' At least with Fenna she can set the record straight. There's a hint of resentment in her tone, she can't deny it, for what Fenna threw at her, months ago, about her son. 'Think what you like, but it's not true, any of it,' she snaps.

'I know,' Fenna says, with an empathy that unsettles her.

'They don't want me any more . . . at work,' Karolina admits, dropping her guard. Perhaps she just needs to talk, confide in someone about how things are really going. 'Too much talk about me, they say. They don't want any trouble.'

'I thought so.'

The conversation could have ended there. But now it's Karolina who keeps it going. 'And you?' she asks, tentatively.

'I've got a job again.'

'Good.'

'Waitress in a bar,' Fenna explains with a chuckle. 'Better than nothing.'

'Right . . .'

'I should have called you sooner, I know,' Fenna admits, to Karolina's surprise, just when she isn't expecting much else from this phone call.

'Maybe if you'd lost your job again . . .' she says sarcastically.

Even though she's not standing in front of her, she can tell Fenna is taken aback. Then she apologises again. 'I just wanted to say I'm sorry. That photo of you in the paper . . . It'll all be fine.'

'Fine, yeah.'

'Jesus, Karolina, spit in my face or something! Call me a bitch!'

'I thought about it. Now it doesn't matter any more.'

'You hate me. I didn't call you before, when that story came out … and now you hate me.'

'No.'

'You hate me!'

'No.' Then she calls her out. 'You've been drinking again.'

'No,' Fenna lies. 'I was upset. For you.'

'I was upset, too.' Karolina says it with spite. The idea that her son Andreas doesn't even exist in a corner of the thoughts of the person she'd always considered her best friend offends her. It would have been far better if Fenna had thrown all the shit she could at her.

'Let's wait until this is done and then get together,' says Fenna. 'It's always like this. A complete clusterfuck, and then it's all over.'

'All over, right.'

'It's bullshit, this story, I know … I just wanted to tell you that,' Fenna concludes. But she doesn't hang up. After a brief silence, she chances the question she shouldn't ask. 'That boy, I mean—'

'What boy?' Karolina stops her, pretending not to follow. In truth, she has no intention of replying.

'Okay. You're right. This is not the time. When we see each other, maybe.'

The voracious curiosity that Karolina perceives in these words, and which her friend clearly cannot hide, leaves a bitter taste in her mouth.

'Listen, as I've got a job now. Do you need anything?' Fenna tries to salvage the conversation.

'No,' is Karolina's response. It's the only thing she feels she can say without ending up even more humiliated and offended.

*

She's back home, sitting at what used to be Andreas's desk, when she feels the rage bubbling up. Maybe it's because her reflection in the black computer screen looks so mournful, but she doesn't waste a second in transforming a nasty thought into a few choice words designed to hurt.

She knows Fenna will answer her call straight away, shocked, or just surprised, that Karolina is ringing back after barely a couple of hours.

She'll cut to the chase, too. No niceties. It will be hard for her to say the words, she knows that, but she so badly wants to spew her rage in Fenna's face, everyone's face, that she's prepared to go that far.

Waiting until she hears, 'Hello, it's you!' and then a second of silence, she says what she's decided to say: 'Yes, it's me. Earlier . . . I wanted to tell you . . .' She takes a calculated pause. 'That my son, you know, Andreas, is dead.'

She doesn't wait to hear the dismay in Fenna's voice. She'd decided that, too. She wasn't going to let her say a word, no comments, no participation.

Only once she's hung up does she realise, and feel horrified by, what she has done – not to Fenna, but to her son Andreas. She can't let herself stop searching for him, even if she doesn't know how or where to find him, and now she is hopelessly, irredeemably alone.

45

Po valley, Emilia-Romagna, 23 January

None of the boys says a word about the expedition to Orso's house. Rambo's line had been clear. Only say as much as it takes to get the old guys off their arses and round to Orso's house. To keep him busy for as long as necessary.

'Necessary for what?'

'Necessary,' Rambo had said enigmatically. 'Not one word more. Not one less,' he had added, referring to the conversation they had to strike up with the older men.

'The other day, we went to do an inspection,' Lele begins, standing at the bar. He looks at Rambo to check whether he is on the right track.

'And?'

'And, it's like he says,' Lele goes on, nodding towards Mr Christmas, who has been coming to the bar for a while now, to see how this thing with the dead child turns out. After all, his house is the most exposed. Exposed to what, he's not exactly clear himself, but the danger is there. No doubt about it.

'And what does he say?' the bar owner enquires, with his usual bad habit of saying slightly too much.

'If you don't believe us, go and see for yourselves,' Rambo butts in, leaving an eloquent silence in his wake.

Reporting the incident to the police isn't even discussed.

'First, we'll find out what's going on, and then countermeasures can be taken. One step at a time.' This is their unanimous stance, led by those who had grandsons or great-grandsons involved in the incident at the camp that went up in smoke on New Year's Eve, with the flames taking a little girl, her grandmother, and dogs, so many dogs. If Orso talked, they'd all be in trouble.

'Right, we'll go and find out what's going on!' concludes the oldest man, who knows Orso better than anyone. 'But just me, him and him,' meaning the ones who could strike up an amicable conversation. 'Sensibly,' he adds, because it's clear that, with Orso, you have to tread carefully. That's why the delegation includes the best drinker who, when he's sober, knows how to talk things through.

Orso is in the shed when, in the early afternoon, he spots a car a few hundred metres away. He soon realises it's the old guys from the bar, heading for his house.

'You stay hidden here,' he says to the child, locking the shed door and whistling for Lupo to follow him, without making a fuss. He ties him to the post near the dog house. 'Get in there!' he orders, to make it clear he shouldn't make a sound.

When the three men had got into the car, the last thing they'd expected to see when they arrived was Orso happily standing on the doorstep. Just the fact that the door is open seems like a good sign.

Even though they're concentrating on how to start the conversation, as soon as they get out of the car and walk towards him, it's clear to all three that Orso is in an unprecedented good mood. He greets them in a way that isn't exactly friendly, but is less rude and gruff than usual. No harshness in his voice. Even his face seems less leathery.

They spend the first half an hour chatting: the weather that's finally getting better; the holidays, that when they're over it's always too late – too many lunches, too many dinners, too much money thrown away, too much stuff, blood sugar, triglycerides, grandchildren, who are a joy, but all of them together for so many days do end up pissing you off.

'So then?'

Orso's question kills the conversation like a gunshot. They've drunk a couple of glasses, which he generously refilled. A proper Lambrusco.

'So then?'

The conversations they'd all gone over in their minds on the way there fall apart, leaving just awkward words. Then the oldest man collects his thoughts and begins.

'We've got grandchildren: you understand, don't you? It's not good to have cameras at school, in the gym, in the toilet, so a person ... a person can't even take a shit in peace. And if they had to take measures like that, it means there's a danger. Nobody can afford to go around doing whatever they like ...' He weighs his words carefully, alluding to what Orso might be up to in his own house. And, if the CCTV cameras showed nothing, no suspicious movements, it meant that there was something else to figure out. And that's what they were here for: to find out, get some answers, look Orso in the eye.

It worries him that the best drinker intervenes before Orso says anything.

'I know what I think. I'm a person with values. But you know that! Everyone knows those people are capable of getting little children mixed up in things ... You've seen them, haven't you? On television. A suicide belt, a little boy sent all bundled up onto a football pitch, and bam! A massacre!'

'Those who?' Orso asks.

'Them, *them*!' the best drinker says. 'You know who we're talking about!'

'Then you should pay a visit to the gypsies,' Orso says sarcastically, as if the camp still existed.

'Where do the gypsies come into it, then?' the oldest man asks, unable to see where Orso is going.

'I'd say they come into it,' Orso continues to bait them. 'Someone should get the police involved.' The way he stresses it, it sounds an awful lot like a threat.

'And since when have you cared about the police?' the oldest man asks.

The one of the three whose grandson was involved in the incident with the fire, and the little girl and her grandmother who died, burnt to a cinder, doesn't want to play Orso's game. He feels a burst of pressure that might kill him. 'If you're referring to our boys,' he blurts out, 'you're wrong. They mess around, shoot their mouths off. That's it. You know what kind of shit there is in there . . .'

'What's with you defending the camp all of a sudden?' the oldest man picks up again. Now he wants to get to the bottom of this, find out which side Orso is on.

'I don't give a shit about the camp. Or about *his* grandson.' Orso's curt response is followed by a fierce glare at the man who brought up the subject of the fire, and who, with his head sunk into his shoulders, now seems to be shrinking under the table.

'So you're on our side? I mean . . . we can count on you, right?' the oldest man concludes, his tone a mixture of fear and shame.

Orso doesn't ask, 'To do what?' He concentrates on what he wants to make clear to them all. 'Tell the *boys* . . . to stay away from my house.' He pours one last glass of Lambrusco to put an end to the matter.

*

That Rambo and his friends have taken advantage of his chat with the 'senile' old folk to break open the door to the shed, Orso only realises when the three men have finally fucked off.

The first thing he thinks is how much of a dick he's been to trust them. Then he rushes to the shed, now reduced to a bombsite. He tries to barge his way through the sea of stuff that hampers every step. Since he doesn't know what to call the child, struggling with his arthritic legs, he runs to Lupo's kennel. 'Find him!' he shouts, giving the dog a kick that makes him yelp.

He can't believe that Lupo, instead of going to the shed, skulks off into the house, whimpering.

'Piece of . . .!'

The words catch in his throat. The child is sitting in his armchair by the fire, with his legs dangling and Lupo hiding underneath.

He's intently reading something on a piece of paper and, when Orso gets closer, he puts it back in the pocket of his shorts.

Since he doesn't really know what to say, or do, the old man picks up a pair of corduroy trousers and a sweater, several sizes too big, which he'd managed to recover this morning from what was left of the Roma camp. The only way he could think of finding something warm for 'the boy' to wear, without getting noticed. That's what he's calling him now.

'It's cold. You'd better put these on,' he says, holding them out at a safe distance so as not to scare him, especially after the fright he must have been given by those pricks. Rambo and his gang in cahoots with the old boys!

46

Palermo, 23–24 January

It had taken Inspector Vitale a while before he'd done the only thing he could do. Having grabbed hold of the boy, picking him up and whispering in his ear, 'You're okay now ...', he couldn't really do anything but knock him out. Keeping him quiet any other way would have been impossible.

It hadn't been easy to get home, with the kid hoisted over his shoulder, dragging the suitcase with his other hand. And he was scared. It was the middle of the night, sure, but someone might still see him.

With his heart thumping, he waited until the lift reached the ground floor, cursing the nerve-rackingly slow countdown as the LED light moved from one floor to the next. Only when he stepped inside the metal cabin and pressed the button did he feel safe. Sliding his key into the lock, quickly closing the door behind him and depositing the boy on the sofa, had tested his nerves to the point of exhaustion.

Then he typed a message to the cleaning lady. He'd completely forgotten that the next day was Sunday. It didn't matter. The important thing was to make sure she didn't turn up at the house for a few days.

'I'm going away. Something's come up at work. See you in the middle of next week.'

Reading it back, before he dropped the phone on the table, he wondered why he'd given himself so much time. 'It's for the best. At least I can relax for a while,' he told himself, flopping into an armchair to keep an eye on the boy.

If he hadn't knocked him out, he'd probably have bitten his hand, he thinks, trying to justify himself. On the other hand, the kid had already tried to sink his teeth into him. It hadn't gone well.

Gripped by worry that wouldn't let up, Inspector Vitale got back out of the armchair. He started pacing around the room. For now, the first thing he had to do was go to the wardrobe and fetch the lost hat he'd picked up at Termini Station on Christmas Eve.

When the boy woke up, it should be immediately clear that Inspector Vitale knew who he was dealing with.

'That's that done,' he tells himself, resting it carefully on the edge of the sofa, trying to keep at bay a thought he really wanted to banish completely, that went a bit like this: why had he brought him home, instead of handing him over like he should have done, and him an officer of the law . . .?

Sometimes we do things that have no logic: that was the only sensible explanation he could find for what he was only just starting to realise was a very foolhardy action.

At three in the morning, Khaled was still on the sofa unconscious, or sound asleep.

Inspector Vitale was struggling to fight sleep. In the end, he gave up. His eyes closed and the boy was back there, perched on the television. Turning to stare at him from unfathomable depths, he started to laugh. A coarse laugh. With a jump, the inspector was awake and his bewildered eyes were scanning the room for the boy with the suitcase. He was still there, lying on the sofa, in the same position he'd left him in a few hours ago.

Perhaps because sleep had clouded his thoughts, or because of the recurring nightmare, now he couldn't get the suspicion out of his mind that the boy might have died. Without leaving the armchair, the solid reality of the leatherette upholstery he was sitting on, he focused on the apparently lifeless body. Seeing the jacket move up and down at chest height in a gentle, slow, rhythmical movement reassured him.

That boy must be very thin. He could tell from the way his trousers flapped loosely around his legs. If they'd been bare, they probably wouldn't have looked much different to the other kid's skinny legs, which had, at some point, been dangling in front of his TV screen.

The expression on this one's face was hard, maybe arrogant, the opposite of the disarmed fragility that was part of what had left him standing frozen in the middle of the room on that fateful night, unable to move a muscle.

He's wondering, 'What now?' again, when the boy stretches out on the sofa. He opens his eyes and looks at him. Maybe he's frightened. The fact is he's staring at him, without moving a muscle, almost waiting for something terrible to happen, some irreparable thing he can't defend himself against.

Inspector Vitale really hadn't expected him to suddenly leap off the sofa and, quickly scouring the room with wild eyes, hurl himself towards the suitcase.

Slowly, he stands up, too, but when he starts to move forward, Khaled pulls the scissors out of his pocket and shows the blade. He is clearly ready to strike.

For a moment, Inspector Vitale weighs up what to do. Then,

taking the boy by surprise, he pulls his police-issue gun from his holster.

'Drop the scissors,' he says, nodding his head down. 'On the ground! Put them down!'

He waits for the boy to understand what he's trying to get across, adding an absolutely unambiguous hand gesture. Then, when Khaled finally decides to let the scissors go, he stretches out a foot to pull them towards him.

'Now we're getting somewhere,' the inspector says to himself.

Wanting to proceed with a clear head, he tries to get his thoughts in order. First, he needs to understand what's in the suitcase that's so important.

'Put that suitcase down,' he says, in the voice of someone giving an order loud and clear. An order that Khaled doesn't register.

The boy pulls the suitcase closer and hugs it even tighter. He looks desperate now. He's almost in tears. He shakes his head.

Again, Inspector Vitale does something he would never have imagined. He approaches the boy and points the pistol between his eyes.

Khaled senses that it's all over. He slowly moves his arms and leaves his suitcase, defenceless, naked in the middle of the room.

He doesn't say, 'Please,' he doesn't beg, but that's what it feels like.

If, before that night, someone had asked Inspector Vitale whether he'd ever experienced true horror or immeasurable shock, he probably wouldn't have known what to say.

Now, after seeing what he'd seen, opening that suitcase that he'd brought into his home like any other piece of luggage, for him, horror and immeasurable shock were embodied by what he now found in front of him, things he could never possibly have imagined: the nauseating, bittersweet stench that hit his throat, the bandages that stank of bodily fluids and camphor wrapped around that thing with the mummified features of a child.

That horror and shock, which was beyond words, leaving the inspector speechless and bewildered, Khaled answered with one stilted phrase, spoken in a language reminiscent of Italian, but which sounded like something all its own, a shapeless mass of pain: 'My-brother-Nadir . . .'

47

Brussels, 24 January

She'd known that there would be a demonstration in the European Quarter that morning. Who was organising it, Karolina wasn't entirely sure, and she hadn't bothered looking into it. A protest against the 'glass palaces' is how it was presented.

She hadn't slept a wink for days, since first the federal and then the local police, with absolutely no coordination, had informed her of the latest findings in their investigations.

'We have evidence that the boy in question has arrived in Italy. The case is being handled by our Italian colleagues. But please don't go anywhere. You can't leave the country for any reason.'

'As if I could. I'm stuck here,' she would have replied, if she'd had a bit more presence of mind.

Regarding her son Andreas, it had been the local police who showed up, after months. It seemed they'd found the T-shirt and maybe also the sweatshirt he'd been wearing that day, close to the Charleroi canal, and a pair of trainers. Not on the quai des Charbonnages side, in the Molenbeek area, they explained, but on this side of the canal, on boulevard de Nieuport, not far from Porte de Flandre. 'What now?' Karolina asked, unable to voice the other terrible question that had hit her about Andreas's fate.

'Now we have some evidence, we can start piecing things together,' they told her abruptly. The case was probably destined to be archived soon.

'It may even be suicide, madam.' It had been good of them to use their 'compassionate' voice, thought Karolina sarcastically.

The truth is that Karolina received the news with a sense of foreboding she couldn't shake off. It was quite a leap to reach her conclusion, but that didn't make the shock of it any less violent: that it was too late to find any traces of her son, wherever he might have ended up, whatever he might have done to himself, or had done to him.

That was the same place (unless she was mistaken) where, some time ago, she'd seen frighteningly huge graffiti, a giant scene. On the wall of a red brick building that now looked black, there was a hand gripping the blade of a knife, while another held down a boy's head by the neck, his eyes closed, his mouth red, his face ashen. Only afterwards she'd noticed that from a side wall, a kind of neighbouring turret, an arm seemed to come straight out of the bricks, and a hand blocked the wrist to stop the blade landing on the boy's throat. Some sort of reproduction of *The Binding of Isaac*, she'd read somewhere when she was trying to understand it. She'd had trouble getting that scene out of her mind, the whiteness of the hands and arms stained with red, and that black blade, an impossible oblique cut. Even suspended like that, it hurt.

That's why she'd decided to go to the protest, to stop that sense of foreboding from winning. She's not interested in other people's reasons for being there. It's for her son, to find out what happened to him, that she's going to stand outside the glass palaces. She would even have gone on her own. She's carrying a plastic bag containing a sheet of cardboard tied to a string. She'll put it round her neck to make her point.

There aren't many people on the metro that Sunday morning, despite the kind of sunshine that isn't hot but tempts you out of the house, even if it's just to take a walk.

At first, she thinks she'll get off the metro at Schuman. Then she opts for Maelbeek.

Rue de la Loi seems even wider and longer than normal. The sky splits it in half, reflected in the geometric glass windows that seem to make life look well regulated. Carrying her bag, and gripped by anxiety, Karolina walks towards boulevard Charlemagne. There aren't many people there, either. No gathering. Perhaps the demonstration has been cancelled, and she didn't know. No matter. She's there now. And it's a nice day. The air isn't as cold. Someone might stop to read the sign she's about to put around her neck, her plea for help.

She's never set foot in the Berlaymont building. She doesn't even know what it's like inside, with its 200,000 square metres of glass and steel. She can't really imagine it. She only knows that before the renovations some officials had died. Pulmonary fibrosis. Tonnes of asbestos inside tonnes of steel. Now nobody's dying here any more. 'Thank God,' she thinks. Because it's not like her to make cruel, indiscriminate jokes, even though she is angry with everyone: a thousand different police units – local, federal, special, integrated – that have followed trails, constructed charges and dismantled them; the journalist who wrote that piece under her stolen photo, making out they knew everything when they knew nothing; the owner of the estate agency who believed it; her potato-headed ex-husband who had dropped off the radar; her friend Fenna who shouldn't have done what she did, betraying her like that. She's also mad with her son Andreas, for leaving her the way he had, without a word, no door slammed in her face, no sign. Not once had he told her where he was going, or what he was doing.

An insignificant speck of nothing in front of something vast. That's how Karolina feels about herself, wrapped in her yellow raincoat, as she approaches the colossal facade of the building: a wave of glass and blue flags dotted with stars, and her, walking up to the headquarters of the European Commission. No more than a bright yellow speck in the milky sunlight.

If the square hadn't been deserted, maybe it would have made sense to put the sign around her neck. One of the protesters would have noticed it, maybe even joined her in her exasperated plea for help. But now that she's in the very spot where she thought she could make her voice heard, in big red letters on white paper, she's struck by a sense of shame. Poor crazy woman with a sign around her neck. It wouldn't be much different to walking up to the few people who are around and saying, 'My name is Karolina. I've lost my son. Nobody will listen to me.' They would give her a funny look and then continue on their way. Maybe someone would be frightened of her, this disconcerting presence getting in their way. The only difference is that, if she put that sign around her neck, after a while the police would probably intervene and move her on. Ah, the police! Always the police! Her mouth twists into a smile.

With the sign wrapped up in her bag, Karolina sits on one of the marble benches installed for people to take a break or eat a quick sandwich outside the Berlaymont building. She puts the bag down at her feet. She looks at the tall cylinders: blue, strawberry pink, orange, bright green, the writing saying BRUXELLES-SCHUMAN that runs vertically down each one of them. Four cylinders that look like they were made in a Lego factory, specifically to enchant small children. 'Please. Don't be dead,' she finds herself muttering quietly, into the void she already knows she's inside, a void so immense that it gives her the feeling, by its very enormity, that she can depend on something: a silent, shadowy presence. 'Please, Andreas-my-son.'

So focused is she on this intimate conversation that she doesn't notice the boy walking towards her. She just has a sudden sense that she can see a white flame. The sun crashing down out of nowhere.

48

Po valley, Emilia-Romagna, 24 January

The air is heavy at the bar that Sunday morning, which seems like a regular work day, anonymous and grey. Like so many others, in the winter, in the valley.

The artificial light casts a vague, uniform glow over the place, barely altering the gloom enveloping them all. If it had already been the afternoon, nobody would have cared; in fact, it would have helped to create the cosiness that usually gives a welcoming feeling to the big, empty room with so little furniture: a few Formica tables, twenty or so rush-bottom chairs and, in a corner, an arcade game, blades and laser guns that seem to have appeared there from the future, or maybe from the past, given that the game is several years old now. It's fashionable for bars to have 'slots to make some money' these days, explained the barman, who was working on getting one for his own place.

Making the atmosphere even heavier than normal are the unusual silence and the stony faces.

The truth is that the old boys are angry with Rambo and his mates for betraying them. The ransacking of Orso's outhouse was an affront to their group. They don't like being taken for the sort of people who would abuse someone's trust, people with no dignity. It was Lele who'd let the cat out of the bag. Without thinking, he'd given a candid response to Mr Christmas, who wanted to know how their errand had gone.

'What errand?' the oldest man interrupted, suspicious of what this question was alluding to. 'What the hell do you mean "a fucking mess all for nothing"?' he yelled at Lele, who was incapable of inventing anything off the top of his head without Rambo there to prompt him.

The oldest of the old men then jumped out of his seat. This business of breaking into Orso's shed, it was a really lousy thing to do, and they'd taken it personally. 'For what?' he started shouting. 'A prank?'

That had happened the previous night at the bar. If glasses and bottles hadn't been thrown, it was only thanks to the intervention of the best drinker, who, already a little hazy, had said, 'Tomorrow morning, tell that Rambo to be here. These things should be discussed with a clear head. If he doesn't show up ...' he took another swig to buy himself some time, 'if he doesn't show up, we'll go and get him ourselves. And there'll be hell to pay. Absolute hell,' he added, slurring his enigmatic finale.

On Sunday morning, however, Rambo isn't there. Nobody knows where he is.

'He's not at home. I asked his mother,' Lele says, arriving with the other boys, ready to kick off if a fight ensues.

The oldest man just looks them all up and down. 'Sooner or later, he'll show up.' Without another word, he starts to sip his coffee, a bottle of grappa on the table, shuffling cards with a calm that leaves the younger men baffled.

Apart from that, nothing much happens. Scores are left unsettled. That is clear to everyone.

*

Orso jumps out of bed and the sun is already high. He'd spent almost all night thinking about what had happened that evening. He'd gone over the scene so many times that, in the end, he was almost afraid it had been a dream, something that had grown, or been leavened, in his mind.

The moments that preceded what he considers his deepest secret – something he could never tell anyone, apart from his wife, Cesira – those moments are just a vague memory, a series of sensations: the silence and the gentle crackle of the fire in the hearth; the heat that spread into the room like a bubble, and inside that bubble were him, Lupo and the child. Everyone in their place, trying to do something: sleeping, watching the red embers, putting away the dishes after dinner. Outside there was a clear moon. Even the snow, flat and endless over the valley, had something of a lunar quality.

In that peaceful, domestic moment, Orso had gone back to look at the lump that was spoiling the child's face. It was now a hard scab, a long crust that must be painful, or maybe unbearably itchy. More than once, he'd caught the child with his little hand up to his face, trying to scratch it off.

As gently as possible, and in truth very clumsily, Orso tried to approach the sofa where the child was sitting. He had a small green bottle in one hand and, in the other, some cotton wool.

'This won't sting,' he said, showing the boy the disinfectant. He might even have arranged his face into a smile, but a cautious, embarrassed one. Smiling was one of those things he'd never been very comfortable with. But yes, maybe he had really smiled, because the child's face lit up. The eyes mainly. Dark and velvety.

It was that light generated between them that gave Orso the courage to lean over and examine the lump better. Pain and itching. He'd experienced that. On his own forehead. That pain and unbearable itching that must be tormenting the child. So he sat down with him on the sofa. He poured the disinfectant onto the cotton wool.

'Gently does it, eh?' he said, moving his hand towards the scab. And the child let him do it. He lifted his head and, pushing it against the back of the sofa, entrusted it to Orso's hands, which were very rough, maybe too rough. He had to be careful.

'It'll be the arthritis,' he thought. He must have lost all feeling in his fingers. As he wiped the cotton wool over the child's face, keeping his head back, he couldn't feel the warmth of the skin under his fingers, or the fragile bone of the jaw. But the lump was gradually thinning down to a long, deep wound that the old man dabbed gently.

'Now, that's better,' he said softly, at last, pleased with the job he'd done. The child's face was now a nice, clean oval, framed by hair straightened at the front and a bit wet from the disinfectant that the old man had used to clean everything up properly.

The thought that the child will have been up for hours and waiting for him in the kitchen forces him out of the bedroom as he is, in the woolly jumper and long johns he puts on every night before he goes to sleep.

He is surprised not to find him on the camp bed that he'd set up in the warmest part of the house, not far from the fire, where the embers are now almost all out. Lupo is nowhere to be seen either.

Orso guesses that they could be outside, in spite of the grey sky that not a single ray of the high sun can permeate, when he sees that the front door is ever so slightly ajar.

Rambo surprises him as soon as he steps outside, trying to catch sight of the child, and Lupo.

'It's just you and me now,' Rambo says, squaring up to him. He doesn't have any weapons on him. Only the knuckleduster, which always comes in handy in a scrap. He's decided to teach the old man a lesson. Settle the score with kicks and punches, aimed where they will hurt the most. Without killing anyone. Just so Orso will remember, for as long as he lives, what Rambo is capable of with his bare hands.

The punch that lands right in the old man's face is only the beginning. Orso is unarmed and half naked. He looks at him, stunned. Then Rambo goes in hard, with volleys of punches; he doesn't even need to worry about dodging the jabs that Orso doesn't throw. The old man just takes it, staying firmly on his feet at first, and then swaying suddenly when Rambo gives him a kick in the middle of the thigh. Knocking him down and beating him even harder, in the head, on the back, is a game Rambo dedicates himself to methodically at that point, repeating the words 'rage' and 'cowards', savouring every moment he has to enjoy this opportunity of a lifetime: catching a double-crosser and making them pay.

With his combat boot on the old man's neck, he stands there looking at the spectacle.

'Rambo never gives up. He always comes back to settle the score. You should thank God I went easy on you, old Bear, otherwise you'd be in the other world by now ... Violence and terror. No barrier can stop a skinhead, none!' These are his final words, pronounced over the old man's head, which is bleeding profusely, before he takes off.

49

Palermo, 24 January

'Our job is to make people feel safe, to dispel fear ...'

Once again, those words had come into his mind and Inspector Vitale couldn't remember whether someone had said them in real life or in one of those heroic films he'd loved so much when he was a kid. And still does now.

After gently closing the lid of the red suitcase over the tiny, deathly face, and standing for a few moments, paralysed by the violence of true horror, Inspector Vitale found himself thinking he should never ever have brought that boy into his house. On the one hand, there was the shock clouding his thoughts; there was a duty to proceed according to the law, to take both of them, the suitcase and its owner, and hand them over to the force he'd been honoured to serve for years, with the loyalty intrinsic to the job he had sworn to do. On the other, there was the naked fear of this little boy who, rocking back and forth, unable to still himself, hadn't stopped repeating for a moment, not to the inspector any more, but to himself, 'My-brother-Nadir.'

'Our job is to make people feel safe, to dispel fear ... To dispel fear.'

It is now dawn on a Sunday that promises to be dazzling, the way that only a few winter days can be on the island – unexpected and mythical – and Inspector Vitale is at a loss.

'To dispel what fear? What fear do we dispel?' he keeps asking himself, turning to look at the boy, who is curled up tighter, wishing he could disappear every time the inspector's gaze settles on him. The very fact that, in those moments, Khaled stops his dirge for a second, and then starts back up, as if he's afraid of losing his place, plunges Inspector Vitale into despair. The truth, if he's honest with himself, is that if anyone feels completely lost, it's him.

It's not really a decision that impels him to put on the coat he'd tossed on the floor last night. It's an instinct.

'Let's go,' he says, with the resolve of someone who can't afford to think too much.

Khaled shakes his head. In a last-ditch attempt to do what he has to do, bringing his journey to an end, he takes the piece of paper from his pocket and holds it out gingerly to the inspector.

'I said let's go,' Inspector Vitale says again, plucking it out of his hands and grabbing the suitcase from the table.

'Walk!' He sweeps Khaled up with one arm. Pulling the little suitcase along on its wheels, the inspector goes to the front door, Khaled behind him.

He doesn't need to watch him. He's sure of one thing: as long as the suitcase is in his hands, the boy won't run.

'Get in,' he says when they reach the Panda parked a few blocks away, after he's put the suitcase in the boot with all the scattered papers, an old raincoat and other stuff that should have been thrown away weeks ago.

The fact that the inspector didn't make him hide in the back, but told him to sit in the front seat, strikes Khaled as a good thing. He has no idea where he will end up, and he doesn't know what will become of his brother, Nadir. So he concentrates on the details. And that little gesture of letting him sit in the front – especially in a car that reminds him of the one they used to drive to the sea in with their father, Salim – seems like a good sign. A sign that maybe all is not lost.

He recognises nothing of the old city he'd seen the day before, emerging from the belly of the ship. And there's nothing that looks like the Clearing, where he ended up at some point. The city that stretches out before him seems completely new: streets, buildings, squares, trees growing in the middle of them. It's as if, during the night, the island had changed its skin. Only the light is the same. Perhaps even more intense and brilliant.

If only he could choose, he would stay here with his brother, Nadir. 'The Ghālib brothers, sons of Salim Ghālib,' that's what his grandmother, Samira, used to call them when she wanted to pay them the highest compliment, always using her most solemn tone.

The last time anyone had called them that was the day they met Padre Buono. This had given Khaled the idea that Padre Buono must know his grandmother, or at least his family, and that's why he was happy to help them out. He'd been disappointed to learn that everyone 'in the construction business' knew Padre Buono, but that he didn't really know anyone.

The Ghālib brothers who go together to buy ice cream from Mr Ahmad al-Haddad. The Ghālib brothers who head off to the nearby field in the afternoons, one in front with a ball tucked under his arm, the other running behind. The Ghālib brothers who sit at the table, each in his own place, and never fight about it. The Ghālib brothers who absolutely must leave. 'Why?' 'Because that's how it is, Khaled.' His mother's voice on the verge of breaking at any moment. Her eyes burning. And his grandmother, Samira, already saying the evening prayer. The Ghālib brothers who don't sleep the whole night, when the day no one wanted to come arrives. The Ghālib brothers who get up at first light and prepare for the journey. 'When are we coming home?' 'Soon, very soon.' 'But when, exactly?' 'When everything's over.' 'When's that?'

It has been so long since Khaled thought about himself and Nadir like this, like his grandmother, and like his father, Salim, when he would put his hands on their heads on a Sunday morning and say, 'We're going out.' It had been nice to feel one of those wide palms on the back of his neck as they walked together down the street, his father in the middle, with the two boys on either side. The way his father, Salim, would hold their hands.

The city has long since disappeared when Khaled detaches himself from the thoughts he's been lost in for a good hour and, looking up, goes back to focusing on the road.

Now he's afraid again. A new fear that makes him dance in his seat, in the throes of an anxiety he can do nothing to contain.

The car vibrates and dances, too, speeding down a road that runs straight through a landscape of rolling hills, rows of vines twisting through wild herbs, patches of brown dotted with green, and farmhouses that look like lone teeth sprouting from the ground.

The piece of paper that the inspector had snatched out of his hand is now open on the dashboard. The red circles and writing are hard to make out in the reflections from the sun-drenched windscreen.

Khaled would like to put it back in his pocket, open the window, escape. Why doesn't this guy do the same as the last one, Omar's friend the secret agent? Why doesn't he stop the car and leave him in the middle of the road, with his suitcase and Nadir?

'The Ghālib brothers, the Ghālib brothers, the Ghālib

brothers . . .' Again he repeats it over and over in his head. Only now he can't go back there, to where every fibre of his being wants to be. That constant grinding of his brain is like a cage within another cage that vibrates and dances on the never-ending road that just keeps unrolling.

The sea, when it finally appears in the corner of the windscreen, is just a patch. Khaled can't even believe that that blue fingernail can really be sea.

50

Brussels, 24 January

The colossal wing of the glass palace is perfectly intact following the explosion. Even the blue flags still have all twelve gold stars in place. Not a tear or a scrap of cloth out of place; nothing has dropped to the foot of the steel flagpoles.

Of Karolina, however, there is very little left, and that little is dispersed among fragments of metal and rubble: indistinguishable human remains.

The mixture of bolts and acetone peroxide, 'Mother of Satan' as it's known, had also done its work on the body of the person who'd activated it. The nothing that remained of the sole attacker had merged with the nothing that was left of Karolina on a section of the shiny pavement outside the Berlaymont building: an extensive stain but ultimately localised, it became clear once the exact area affected by the explosion was cordoned off.

Something must not have gone according to plan. That's the first conclusion. Apart from the fear, the risk involved, the narrowly avoided massacre, all things considered, the damage was limited. 'It could have been a bloodbath ...' but there was just one victim, explained the journalist sent to the scene. A middle-aged Belgian woman who just happened to be there, probably enjoying a spot of sunshine on a Sunday afternoon. And that 'she should chance to find herself faced with the blind fury of indiscriminate violence, especially in the shadow of such a symbolic building ...' said the journalist, crafting his words live, must lead us to question the effectiveness of security measures, border controls, the ultimate solidity of a Europe 'that has just seen an attempt made on its very heart', he concluded, indicating the facade of the Berlaymont building, before adding the human angle, which it was impossible to ignore and which struck him as the best way to wrap up his first broadcast. Everyone could identify with 'that Belgian woman', who, in her own way, was a kind of symbol, 'a symbol of all ordinary people exposed to threats and dangers from outside Europe's borders.'

Words that would echo in the minds of many, even that same freelance journalist who, a few weeks after the attack on the European Commission headquarters, would try to publish an account of the 'ordinary life' that, before it ended the way it ended, had – he had discovered – been, 'turned upside down by an extraordinary twist of fate'. The woman had died by chance, of course, but she hadn't been there by chance. This was the conclusion he reached after a hard struggle to obtain information about her; his enquiries had been met with reticence and unexplained silences.

When he'd started work, mistakenly convinced that he could finish the piece in a few days, he could never have imagined that all the papers he worked for would just shove his file into a drawer. It didn't add anything significant to the investigation. It risked fuelling pointless controversies. It transformed this woman – whose fate had moved the entire nation, Europe, the international community – into a problem; it was the last thing they needed. These were more or less the reasons.

What the freelance journalist was not inclined to write a single line about were the final moments of 'Lady Karolina', as he'd called her in that piece: whether she'd realised what was happening, whether she'd seen anything, whether she'd had time to think about her son, Andreas, who'd vanished into thin air.

About the attacker, in the end, they knew very little: that he'd been a child; that he'd come from Italy; that he'd been in trouble with the law; that he'd had contact with terrorist groups based in Belgium for no more than a month – his radicalisation had been quick; that he was an example of what it meant to allow fanatics like that to go around unchecked; that his name had been Omar.

If Karolina hadn't been so focused on her silent prayer, sent out to the only person she still expected anything from, she probably would have, if not understood, at least heard the final words spoken by that boy, determined to do his duty, even though there wasn't so much as a dog in sight. He wasn't going to be taken for a fool! So, after a moment's hesitation in view of the unexpectedly deserted area, he'd walked straight towards the woman sitting alone in front of the Berlaymont building.

If Karolina hadn't been so focused, perhaps she might have sensed the rage the boy was in as he walked in front of her, without even looking her in the eye, saying, in the tone of someone who feels betrayed, 'Now we'll see who's the God of gods who speaks all the languages on Earth, and makes you listen!'

Or perhaps Karolina had seen him coming in that wild, unbridled rage – who knows? But only right at the end, a second before.

51

Palermo, 24 January

The sea they reach, after a rough walk on bramble-strewn paths that take them through tall mastic trees, euphorbia and broom, deep into golden-yellow fields of wood sorrel, and past rare almond trees flowering too early, is a small bay with a pervasive smell of resin and iodine. A wedge of immaculate water and sand mixed with shingle, enclosed by rocky cliffs – on which caper bushes climb the blades of wild prickly pears – and a small, flat-topped hill.

It hadn't been easy pulling the suitcase that far. Midway, Inspector Vitale had had to carry it in his arms, taking care not to slip on the unpaved path, the last section of which dropped straight down to the bay. Khaled almost fell several times, finding precarious handholds in tufts of grass and spindly branches that had just enough give. The closer he got to the sea, the more uneasy he felt about this silence broken by the lightning calls of birds he couldn't see.

The boat appeared from behind a rock once they were on the beach. A deep purr and suddenly the red and blue of a prow. They only spotted the driver as the boat, too bright to seem real, began heading slowly towards the shore. Now, it was there, almost aground on the low seabed, waiting.

The words Inspector Vitale exchanges with the sailor, who looks like the captain of a vessel much larger than this fishing boat, are few and, to Khaled, incomprehensible. That this is the person whose name Padre Buono had circled in red, Khaled gathers from the way the inspector holds out the paper that says the exact place Nadir has to go.

He doesn't know whether to move away from the suitcase – which the inspector has left in the sand to go and meet the man on the boat – or whether to stay there. Then he thinks of something he needs to do. He takes off his shoes, rolls up his trousers the way the inspector did and wades into the water.

From his jacket pocket, he pulls out the money his friend Omar gave him, and hands it to the man.

When Khaled and Inspector Vitale go back to the shore together to fetch the suitcase, which is standing alone, leaning slightly in the sand, they notice something that neither of them would ever be able to explain, and which the captain standing on the boat doesn't seem to see, or perhaps he doesn't care.

From the other side of the hill, in the silence broken only by the lone cries of birds Khaled still can't see, something seems to be arriving. First the heads appear, then bit by bit the bodies.

They come in small groups, in dribs and drabs. Hundreds, maybe thousands of creatures. In the distance, they seem to be made of the same stuff as the cloudless sky above the fields, brambles, bushes, tall grasses, rocks, prickly pears and the flat-topped hill where they all stop. From there, they watch Khaled and Inspector Vitale, who stare back with the same wonder as if they were contemplating a mirage.

The hill is now crowded with bodies, which would be fearsome if it weren't for the ball of sun casting a light without shadows, and seeming to burn the flat surface of the sea with an astral fire.

If the mothers and fathers, uncles and aunts, brothers, sisters and grandparents had been there, they could, if nothing else, have seen their own creatures arrange themselves into one giant, silent wing. A crowd of eyes all pointing at the little bay where the suitcase is waiting for someone to lift it out of the sand and take it to the boat. Inspector Vitale lets Khaled do this himself. 'You have to see things through to the end,' is the only thing he can think. And that's for the best.

Struggling through the sand, where his feet sink in up to his ankles, Khaled carries the suitcase in his arms. If he didn't have to turn his back to the hill, perhaps he would have seen, and recognised, in the middle of the assembled crowd, the features of a boy groping around half blind. In the end, he makes it, too, to the top of the flat-topped hill. He stands slightly apart from the others, but he must not be able to see much. If his cross eyes could make out the beach, he would without doubt raise an arm, to make himself known, or just to greet his friend Khaled, who'd finally made it. Nor must he have seen the woman, who isn't all that far from him, in the yellow raincoat that makes her look like an eccentric, shiny bird. She can't have seen him either, although she's doing nothing but looking around, searching, with the sleepless eyes of someone who can't find peace. All together, though, they make an incredibly dense, compact backdrop. And still more are arriving, all coming over the hill, all silent. From the flat top, they watch Khaled, who enters the water with his cargo in his arms, taking care not to get it wet.

'Come on, make it snappy!'

The impatient voice rises from the sea. Stretching out from the prow, the captain reaches towards Khaled, blinded by the slivers of sunlight reflected on the undulating surface. Comforted, in a way, by that rocking of wood and water, Khaled finally abandons all resistance. He releases the suitcase into the man's arms. Then he gestures for him to wait a moment. He pulls out of his pocket the mother-of-pearl comb that his mother had given him before they left, and hands it to him. 'That way, when he arrives, she'll know it was her son Khaled who made things right,' he surprises himself by thinking.

He has no idea of the immense sigh that, at that precise moment, is released from the hillside. Only Inspector Vitale seems to notice it. In fact, he turns round. Then, as if overwhelmed by the impossible enormity, he turns back to focus on the sea, to watch the last manoeuvres with which the captain raises the anchor, and turns to start the engine.

As the prow reverses course, pointing towards the whiteness of the horizon, no matter how much the stones are hurting his feet, Khaled doesn't move a muscle. He stays in the water as the boat slowly fades to a speck and disappears.

When at last he has to turn round and go back to the shore, where Inspector Vitale is waiting, loneliness descends on him, suddenly and violently.

The hill is now deserted; there isn't a soul on its flat top. The sky is clear. The rocks let the water lap over them as it comes and goes, comes and goes, with a splash that each time leaves behind veils of foam and salt in the gaps between the stones and on the shore, to where Khaled has returned.

He doesn't say a word; he doesn't cry, even though it's by no means easy.

Inspector Vitale looks around, suddenly afraid that someone might see them. He knows it's time to go now. He rolls his trousers down and puts his shoes back on.

Before they set off towards the cliff that awaits them, he doesn't feel he can ignore the confused questions Khaled isn't asking, or perhaps doesn't know how to ask: about his brother, Nadir, in the middle of the sea again; about his mother, who hasn't heard anything for months and is waiting for them; about his home that seems so unreachable that he struggles to even remember what it was like ...

So Inspector Vitale nods. 'He'll get there,' he whispers. What else could he say?

52

Po valley, Emilia-Romagna,
24–25 January

He doesn't know how long he had lain on the ground unconscious, after Rambo had unleashed his final kick, before his
combat boots crunched down the driveway and to his bike, leaving nothing behind but two thick tyre tracks on the dirt road.

Pushing his palms into the floor to steady himself, he manages
to get up. He can put weight on one leg, but the other must be
broken. Bent double from the pain searing through his sternum
and ribs, he drags himself towards the house, even though, at
first, it is a blurred clot swirling around with the shed, the trees
and everything else. He's bleeding from his nose, his split lip, his
cheekbone. Even the back of his neck must have a deep wound.
He only needs to look at the snow to see how hard the guy had
beaten him.

Trying to reconfigure the world as it keeps spinning, he takes
a deep breath, which helps. He calls Lupo, hoping that the child
will appear too.

He waits long enough to know that there's no one out there.
So, limping, he makes his way inside.

He spies Lupo's tail through the open door. And that seems

like a good sign, even though nothing good is happening. Because Lupo might well be dead, seeing as he doesn't come to meet him, or move from under the table, where he must have been trying to hide.

Seeing him raise an ear when he enters the house gives Orso some hope. Maybe the child is hiding somewhere, too, and just waiting until he closes the door, making sure they're safe.

'It's all right. Everything's all right,' he says, leaning back in a chair. Then he manages to reach his rifle and, with the barrel to the floor, leaning on the stock, he tries to walk around, looking for the child, who's nowhere to be found, and Lupo does nothing to help.

By chance, between the covers on the camp bed, he finds the piece of paper that he'd seen 'his boy' holding a few nights ago. It's very crumpled and the edges are torn, but he would be able to read it with the magnifying glass he keeps on the nightstand.

The time it takes to go into the bedroom and back to the kitchen, where he'd left the paper spread out on the table, under the brightest lamp in the whole house, feels like an eternity. But he has no choice.

Fortunately, the words are in Italian, even if the handwriting is ill-formed. It's a kind of identity card that someone put in the child's pocket, who knows when and who knows where. Orso understands from the very first lines.

'My name is Nadir. I am four years old. I am the son of Salim Ghālib. My mother is called Leila. My grandmother, Samira. My older brother, who is here with me, is called Khaled. If I get lost, take me to him.'

When he finishes reading, Orso stays sitting with his hands crossed on the kitchen table, just as he did the night he sat there and wept for his wife until morning.

It's dawn again when he decides what to do.

He dresses himself as best he can. He folds the piece of paper into his pocket, and picks up the rifle. He calls Lupo, who is curled up under the table, heartbroken.

'Let's go and find him!' he says, opening the front door.

Author's Note

This book arose from a question that struck me as extremely urgent: what does it mean to produce literature in dark times?

In recent years, I've come to the conclusion that, to get to the heart of reality, we need to talk about ghosts, nightmares and imaginary truths we believe, or are led to believe, are real.

This is a work of fiction, very slightly dystopian fiction: the story is set in the near future, 2020. But the book also includes information and events from real life, things that really happened, despite how implausible they seem, although some details have been changed.

Below are just some of the sources I used in relation to the real-life facts and figures incorporated or adapted in the book.

The Russian promoter Denis Nikitin, who organises mixed martial arts competitions across Europe, and who created the brand White Rex (whose T-shirts with neo-Nazi symbols and xenophobic slogans such as 'Zero Tolerance' I mention in the novel) really exists. On 20 June 2015, Rome hosted 'Tiger's Den', the third music and MMA competition organised by CasaPound in collaboration with White Rex.

EVELINA SANTANGELO

Here is the interview published by the nationalist newspaper *il Primato Nazionale*, in which Denis Nikitin explains the 'Spirit of the Warrior' that White Rex promotes across Europe through amateur MMA fights. https://www.ilprimatonazionale.it/sport/leuropa-rinasceranel-combattimento-parola-di-white-rex-25283/

White Rex also promotes and supports concerts by German neo-Nazi bands like Moshpit, Brainwash and, in particular, the Russian band You Must Murder (mentioned in the novel). This is discussed in the following articles: http://anton-shekhovtsov.blogspot.com/2014/11/russian-extreme-right-white-rex.html and http://www.antifa.cz/content/what-white-rex

A glimpse into the world of CasaPound: the demonstration in Milan in October 2014; the realities of life in Latina; the reassuring symbol of the salamander on the shirts worn by CasaPound's 'civil protection' units; cage fighting ... all documented in this episode of the TV programme Piazzapulita: https://www.youtube.com/watch?v=wCqvP2eRGOM

The videos mentioned by the Turkish police officer are real. The song 'Death' by the Russian band Slaughter to Prevail can be found here: https://www.youtube.com/watch?v=FPuEDC1sUwA and 'Evil Russia' by You Must Murder here: https://www.youtube.com/watch?v=XktasTjWmNo

All the band names cited are real.

The case of Winzerla and the 'Döner-Morde' ('Kebab Murders'), as they were called in the press, refers to events (attacks and murders of Turkish people, particularly in Nuremberg, Hamburg, Munich, Rostock, Dortmund, Kassel, Heilbronn) that really happened in Germany between 2000 and 2011.

It's true that in 2010 the band Gigi & Die Braunen

Stadtmusikanten released the CD *Adolf Hitler lebt!*, which includes a song called 'Döner-Killer' clearly condoning these crimes.

This is a link to the band's CD released in 2010: https://www. discogs.com/%20Gigi-Die-Braunen-Stadtmusikanten-Adolf-Hitler-Lebt/release/3785382

This is one of the sites where I found information about this case: https://www.glistatigenerali.com/giustizia_terrorismo/una-scia-di-morti-e-feriti-i-neonazisti-tedeschi-vanno-a-processo/

Deso Dogg died in Syria on 17 January 2018. Denis Cuspert alias Deso Dogg alias Abu Talha al-Almani was a successful German rapper and a mixed martial arts fighter who was radicalised and went to fight with ISIS in Syria, and was known for having taken part in many decapitations and becoming one of the leading figures in jihadist propaganda with his violent videos.

His story was told in New York magazine *The Fader*: https:// www.thefader.com/2016/08/02/isis-denis-cuspert-deso-dogg-rapper, and also briefly in this article in *Corriere della Sera*, January 2018: https://www.corriere.it/esteri/18_gennaio_19/deso-dogg-rapper-dell-isis-morto-era-simbolo-gruppo-terroristico-cdfe7262-fcdc-11e7-9ea6-86c42f4fddof.shtml

This video about Deso Dogg inspired the scene where Karolina meets the MMA instructor: https://www.youtube.com/ watch?v=tdEFgZpclVM

The neo-Nazi and jihadist phrases that mix together in Karolina's head when she leaves the gym evoke similar phrases spoken in real life by members of the now disbanded Belgian jihadist network Sharia4Belgium (speech in front of the Atomium in Brussels: https://www.youtube.com/watch?v=cZpYUMTr9KU) founded by Fouad Belkacem (sentenced in 2015 to 12 years in prison; also inspired by online sermons by the Syrian Salafi preacher Omar Bakri Muhammad, who moved to London and is now in Lebanon: https://www.huffingtonpost.it/2015/01/17/terrorismo-mappa-jihad-eu_n_6492446.html) and neo-Nazi claims and speeches such as those made by Flemish neo-Nazi Eddy Hermy and German National Socialist Axel Reitz in January 2010.

The rally held by European neo-Nazi groups in the Flemish village of Moerbrugge not far from Brussels (the first congress of the Nieuw-Solidaristisch Alternatief party, or N-SA) actually happened in 2010. It was attended by some of the most dangerous far right leaders in Europe, and that rally had performances by far right bands from various European countries, Holland, France, Belgium, Italy, Germany . . . including the band Ultima Frontiera from Friuli, who proudly call themselves fascist, and the Dutch radical-nationalist band Brigade M (who played many times for Blood & Honour) with the violently racist, xenophobic, antisemitic and Islamophobic track 'Eigen Volk Eerst' ('Our Own People First') with lyrics about people being on the brink of an abyss and multiculturalism and the mixing of races being a stab to the heart. This was also the scene of talks, which I report some passages from, by Eddy Hermy (who has several suspended sentences to his name) and Axel Reitz (special guest at far right rallies across Europe, candidate for the far right NPD, convicted in Germany of antisemitism and wearing neo-Nazi symbols). This rally was attended by figures like Kris Roman, who in 2009 invited a former Ku Klux Klan leader to Belgium. Or Tim Mudde, once the leader of the now-banned Dutch Centre Party. https://www.youtube.com/watch?v=1xZWVjrhVUE

In the scene where Karolina goes to the rally in Moerbrugge, I changed some aspects of the real-life event: I had it take place on New Year's Eve 2020; I added characteristic elements of particular fringes of the far right in Europe, such as not drinking alcohol or taking drugs; I imagined a girl who chants the names of the most powerful international neo-Nazi organisations she identifies with. Along with the performances by bands that were really there, I had an MMA cage fight take place as well.

The words 'Hammerskins' and 'Blood and Honour' spoken by the girl at the New Year's Eve party refer to neo-Nazi organisations on the global far right. Hammerskin Italia was founded in 1995. (Its nerve centre is in Milan and the surrounding areas in Lombardy. This is where the first European rallies were held: on 28 November 2015, Milan played host to a large rally and concert by Nazi-rock bands to celebrate the twentieth anniversary of its founding). Hammerskin Italia is the Italian arm of Hammerskin Nation, or Fratellanza Hammerskin, one of the world's most organised and violent neo-Nazi and white supremacist networks (established in Dallas in 1988 by a branch of the Ku Klux Klan).

The neo-Nazi network that originated in England, Blood & Honour (which, like Hammerskin, combines politics and Nazi-rock) takes its name and its motto from the Hitler Youth, and preaches the purity of the white race and the violent fight against immigrants and Jews. The organisation was banned some years ago in many European countries, including Germany and Spain. In 2011, the group S.P.Q.R. Skins in Rome sought affiliation to Blood & Honour, intending to open a base in Italy in a house occupied by CasaPound in Colleverde and managed by the group S.P.Q.R. Skins.

The international festival of the Hammerskin community, which takes place every year in Milan, on 19 November 2016 chose the title Europe Awake and was held in collaboration with Blood & Honour. The following articles provide further information: https://ilmanifesto.it/nazi-rock-fuori-tempo-e-tanta-xenofobia-unadunata-milanese/ and https://www.corriere.it/cronache/11_settembre_12/roma-blood-honour_5d233c68-dd2f-11e0-a93b-4b623cb85681.shtml

Karolina's actions and obsessions in the search for her son were inspired by a number of articles, but in particular this report about mothers of foreign fighters published in the *Huffington Post*: https://highline.huffingtonpost.com/articles/en/mothers-of-isis/

To understand how jihadist propaganda works, and also the state of mind of a parent of a foreign fighter, I found it very helpful to listen to this interview with the father of Jake Bilardi, the Melbourne teenager who was radicalised online and died in a suicide bombing in Iraq. Here is the link to the interview from March 2016: https://www.youtube.com/watch?v=HSV8NL5AWLI

For talking about the unexpected and unsuspected radicalisation of young people, their psyches, the repercussions on their families and the presence of a network of recruiters in Europe, including Belgium, I was also inspired by this ABC News interview from 2016: https://www.youtube.com/watch?v=Yz8jpGmhHZ4

The scene with Rambo 2 and his arsenal was inspired by an episode of the TV series Piazzapulita from 2015, 'Veneto Armato', featuring a man in his twenties from Schio, who keeps guns, clubs and knuckledusters in his bedroom: https://www.youtube.com/watch?v=waECQgkdpDQ

Some of the lines spoken by the older men were inspired by another episode of Piazzapulita, 'Veneto Accogliente?', dedicated

to the north-east of Italy. This is the video: https://www.youtube.
com/watch?v=Z8lU974INW8

This link is to the song Khaled sings when he emerges, starving,
from his hiding place in Termini Station in Rome: https://www.
youtube.com/watch?v=zFChKk7Z7s8

Acknowledgements

I've been working on this book for around three years, a period marked by many personal and shared events. Things that seemed like my own weird fantasies about strange movements, strange thoughts, or strange words have become reality, or a nightmare reality, and things I thought could never happen to me have indeed happened. Because that's how books are: they become interwoven with life, with its most unexpected trials and tribulations.

I have many people to thank, and not only when it comes to the actual writing of this novel, but people without whom I probably wouldn't have made it to the end.

First of all, a friend who's like a brother to me, Nino Rotolo, whose help was immeasurable and who deserves my immense gratitude.

And then my extended family, which includes sisters, brothers, cousins, uncles and aunts, nephews and nieces, Bea, my dog Rio, and friends like Gloria Li Brizzi, Marina Mendolia, Letizia di Gaudio, Barbara Crescimanno, Egle Corrado and Maria Antonietta Nigro, who were always there when I needed them.

Thanks also to writer friends (Helena Janeczek, Hamid Ziarati, Chiara Valerio, Marcello Fois, Teresa Ciabatti, Diego

De Silva, Alessandra Sarchi, Valeria Parrella, Rossella Milone, Gian Mauro Costa, Michela Murgia) who 'kept me company' day after day, even at a distance, for so many months, each in their own way.

Thank you to my friend and Middle East expert Paola Caridi, for her quick answers to my rambling questions and for the 'How's it going?' that greeted me almost every day.

One thank you that exceeds the bounds of gratitude goes to my friend Caterina Bonvicini, who did everything: she gave me the right advice at the right time, offered me some peace when I most needed it and gave me a kick when somebody had to. It's no coincidence that we finished our novels in different rooms of the same house, writing the final words of our stories at the same time. Thanks to Riccardo Chiaberge for his unconditional hospitality.

Endless thanks, too, to Paola Gallo and Dalia Oggero, who achieved the impossible by giving me peace of mind, friendship and attention, and for handling this novel with exceptional care and sensitivity.

Thanks to Stefania Cammillini and her messages, to Paola Novarese and everyone who had me in their thoughts, especially those, like Irene Babboni, who were around at the hardest times.

Thanks to Sabina Minardi, who was able to wait for me.

Thanks to Piergiorgio Nicolazzini, for his calmness and clarity.

Thanks to Adele Carriglio, who still wanted to read one of my books when she had so much else to deal with. And thanks to Costanza Quatriglio for those wonderful days.

Thanks to Marina Schembri, who, at the end, ran with me at breakneck speed to get the book finished on time.